Sisters

A PREQUEL TO MESSENGER
SEEN FROM A DIFFERENT ANGLE

MICHAEL POLOWETZKY

ISBN: 978-1-63950-016-1 (sc)
ISBN: 978-1-63950-017-8 (e)

Writers Apex

Gateway Towards Success

8063 MADISON AVE #1252
Indianapolis, IN 46227
+13176596889
www.writersapex.com

To Julie

"I fear not the coming battle"
–Saint Therese of Lisieux

CONTENTS

SOULMATES

....

*A*fter journeying from her quiet, picturesque, baronial estate in the *Lake Country* of Westmorlandshire to sprawling, hectic, busy, metropolitan London, Mary Preston, entirely new to urban life, soon became close friends with nanny Leopoldine Fauré. If the wealthy English duchess and the daughter of a plumber from Rouen, France emerged from varied backgrounds, the two teenagers shared a much deeper, far more important quality. A personal attribute, transcending all national, class, economic and social disparities. Both girls wished to provide a lasting, positive, worthwhile contribution to their troubled world. As yet unsure of how precisely to achieve this lofty goal, each pensive virgin looked to the other as her surest ally and wisest counselor.

This thoughtful duo normally convened their deliberations atop a red wooden bench in *Regent's Park* under a wide evergreen tree. Or, if rain prevented it, the girls continued their heated-discussions inside Westminster Abbey, the *National Gallery,* the *Victoria and Albert,* the *British Museum* or another of London's many historic and cultural monuments. With each succeeding rendezvous, these fiercely-attached friends each became conscience of being in the presence of a fellow-ardent, like-restless, mutually-exploring free-spirit.

In partial recognition of their bond, the two young ladies began dressing in an identical manner. Same: monickered navy blue jacket; tartan skirt; frilly white blouse; wheat-colored chapeau; white bobbysocks and flat black shoes fastened with strap. A similar handbag, too, was slung over each girl's left shoulder. Both wore a large, metal Gothic cross attached to a chain hanging round teenager's neck.

A few weeks later, Leopoldine announced that she was soon returning to France to enter a religious community. "It's not one of those old, anti-Semitic, rattle-off prayers, fumble with beads, light candles and feel holier-than-thou Orders" she explained. "It's quite new."

"New? Is that so?"

"Well, not precisely" elaborated Leopldine. "It's actually the oldest women's religious group of them all. It dates back to the Sixth Century. However, one of its youngest current members was recently given permission to teach the group's message in the larger world."

"I, See. That sounds exciting."

"That's what I meant by describing this as a *quite new Order*. It is one designed to form a place in which modern, liberal, socially-conscious girls like you and I can employ our faith and energies in today's secular world. Those who join are given a chance to truly leave a lasting and positive mark."

"Great!, splendid, just as it should be! What is this new section of the oldest women's group called, Leopoldine?"

"Simply, *The Sisterhood*."

"That sounds straight to the point" observed Mary, approvingly.

"Would you like to accompany me?" soon inquired Leopoldine. "Would you like to come along with me? It'll be awesome, really super, if we can join *The Sisterhood* together!"

Mary pondered for a minute.

A second

Third

"Yes, yes. Awesome, super!" replied the young Duchess of Airandel at last. She pecked her comrade's lips, next, held her soulmate lovingly, close. "Yes! Sure! I'll be most honored to come along with you Leopoldine! That sounds *really* awesome, *really* super! We'll give our lives and our hearts to God's service *together!*"

"Awesome, Mary. We'll serve together!"

"First though, please tell me a bit more about this group and about the lady who founded it."

"Sure Mary. It's quite an interesting story."

FOUNDRESS

"To start with" once recalled Sister Jeanne Navarro to a television interviewer, "I was born on a mountainside. At least six-thousand feet above sea level! From my earliest recollections, I believe looking down on humanity from these lofty heights allowed me to acquire a wider, a more questioning perspective on God's creation."

This was a–worldview, a sense of social duty–the foundress of the group Mary Preston and Leopoldine Fauré embraced, cherished throughout an eventful time on earth. Hers was a–philosophy of life, a feeling of religious obligation–proving to be at once an aid and a hindrance. One, both enhancing ambition and setting obstacles to its achievement. As a result, to some members of the European public, Sister Jeanne and her followers are: "farsighted social theorists and noted theologians." While to others, "these "harpies are dangerous anarchists and inveterate troublemakers." Yet as one of the defining personalities of the last hundred years, the Sisterhood's unique leader–a kid from the provinces who made good–likely would never wish her story to unfold in any other manner.

Feminist; union organizer; foreign correspondent; award-winning, best-selling author; left-wing political theorist; first in her family to graduate from university; Christian—Maria-Juana Navarro was born in a rural community of just three hundred inhabitants halfway-up a mountainside near the French-Spanish border in Ariege Department. Clearly seen in every direction is a magnificent, unforgettable panorama of the snow-capped Pyrenees. On occasion, a solitary wild ibex with massive curving horns, its body covered in a shaggy gray coat, emerges atop one of the steep ridges, an abrupt several thousand meter precipice directly below. Upon it reaching the edge, the ibex stops to gaze-out contemplative–the vista ahead, seeming as impressive to beast as to human being. The range's loftiest peaks, those most difficult to scale except by wild ibex, are covered in white twelve months a year. Not far from the Navarro family home, directly visible from their daughter's bedroom window is narrow, boulder-strewn Roncesvalles, or on French maps: Ronceveaux Pass. Here, in AD 778, the Frank warlord Roland met a death immortalized in epic song. Hannibal, Trajan, Charlemagne, Blanche of Castile, St..Teresa of Avila Napoleon, Goya, Arthur Koestler, Ernest Hemingway and Simone Weil all too, each once passed this way.

Given her place of birth, it should be no surprise Juana Navarro became a maverick. Ariege Department has throughout its history been a region noted for men and women prepared to set off along a nontraditional path. The world-renown Paleolithic *Cave des Trois Freres* at Montesquieu-Avantes, is named for the three brothers who discovered the grotto by chance in 1914. This celebrated natural chamber dating to approximately 13,000 BC is is arguably too where visual art first came into existence. Along the enclosure's winding walls the visitor observes priceless, beautiful, enigmatic Ice Age paintings of religious and magical ceremonies performed by animals and men joined together in mystical reverie. In Roman times, the area was first inhabited by the ever-independent minded Basques. In the Middle Ages, Ariege was a center of the Albigensians or Cathars–an ascetic Christian sect originally from Persia which believed: the Bible was open to individual interpretation; that the purpose of life was to serve others and that all property should be kept in common. The Cathars also rejected the power of the Pope and the clergy; assessed no taxes and considered women equal to men. Nearly all the colorful, romantic Medieval troubadours such as Raymond of Toulouse, Guiraudo de Rios and William of Aquitaine belonged to the Cathar sect. Not surprisingly, these heretics, their lovely ballads or not, soon incurred the ire of the Vatican and were massacred during *The Albigensian Crusade* at Montségur in 1244.

Later, during the *Wars of Religion* in the 1500s, many in Ariege–the descendents of the Cathars–supported the Huguenots. The population which rebelled several times again in the 1600s, as much in the name of regional independence as of Protestantism, found many of their towns and churches plundered by the Grand Condé. In the summer of 1789, the Ariegois became the first outside Paris to cast off the authority of Louis XVI and embrace The Revolution. In the early to mid-1800s, as industrialization came to the region, peasants, fearing the loss of their land and forests to business, waged a long guerrilla fight against the intruders. Because the peasants often dressed as women, the conflict is called *The War of the Maidens.*

Closer to our own era, during the *III Republic* this region along the Pyrenees championed the innocence of Captain Alfred Dreyfus when the vast majority in France, including Emile Zola, still thought him a traitor. Ariege was long represented in the National Chamber of Deputies by the great Socialist leader Jean Juares. Supporters of *The Popular Front* in 1936, many in this Department actively helped the Loyalists in the *Spanish Civil War.* Ariege is too, the birthplace of the famous novelist, playwright and filmmaker Marcel Pagnol, the first movie artist elected to the Académie Francaise. During the 1940s, the word *Maquis* was coined in Ariege.

Until it was finally imposed on the younger generation following *The Great War* by a central government-directed-school system, the population of this often isolated southern region spoke not standard Parisian French but Occitan–a mixture of Sephardic, Catalonian, Gallo-Celtic and Italian. During her lifetime, the words of a person as widely celebrated today as St. Bernadette of Lourdes would be indecipherable to those living in the capital. Occitan was the same dialect employed in the verses of the twelfth century troubadours and spoken by the great queens Eleanor of Aquitaine and her granddaughter Blanche of Castile. As a child of this go-its-own-way land, Juana was very much shaped by local tradition.

More than a mile above sea level, Juana's birthplace: San Pedro (on French maps: St. Pierre) straddles the snaking, meandering, Spanish-French border. Or so, this demarcation winds its way according to

5

governments and cartographers. Like the solitary ibex, this town was present long before Spain, France, or map-making ever existed. The recognized national border in two instances cutting San Pedro/St. Pierre in half, residents consider it a mere artificial line in the dirt. A mere line in the soil wrongfully attempting to divide one closely-tied community possessed of a single history, of a single culture, language and for many of its members, a common bloodline.

Juana was a late and only child. Her parents, also born and raised in this historic area had interesting personal stories of their own. The couple's daughter took from them both an important lesson. Although in each case, it was likely not a teaching either her father or mother expected.

Javier-Diego Navarro was a hero of the French *Resistance*. Unlike many others, who waited to jump on the political liberation bandwagon only after victory for the Allies seemed assured following *D-Day*, Juana's father embraced the patriotic opposition in the dark period of June 1940. A time, when the triumph of Hitler and fascism appeared to all but a brave few, inevitable. "During those frightening early days" Javier later said, "an underground resistance group was exceedingly lucky to survive just three months before it was betrayed. Standing up to the Nazis and the Collaborators was practically a delayed death sentence." Most in his small band (mainly teenagers of both sexes), their names forever unknown, were indeed soon either betrayed or killed outright. By what he claimed to be sheer accident, Javier escaped, though he remained almost constantly on the run. He never slept in one house twice, only traveled at night, a heavy price was on his head. Javier distributed patriotic literature encouraging opposition to the fascists; he participated in many successful sabotage campaigns; operated a clandestine radio which transmitted Axis army maneuvers to Britain; ran a network escorting downed-Allied pilots to safety in neutral Spain.

In early 1943, Javier was transported secretly to London in order to become a special emissary of General de Gaulle. Several months later, he was parachuted back into occupied France armed with both the mission and the authority to establish and direct unity among the dozen or so bitterly-feuding *Resistance* factions. These bands of partisans varied in philosophy from Royalist to Marxist, some were separatist in their ultimate objectives, others internationalist. As in the case of the more famous Jean Moulin, Javier Navarro was soon betrayed. Almost certainly too, by the Communists, who judged a French alliance with De Gaulle posed as great a threat to Stalin and his wider postwar designs as did Hitler. Tortured, he refused to give up names. Sent to Auschwitz, he again, almost miraculously survived. After the end of the war, Javier returned to San Pedro/St. Pierre, sick, emaciated and the haunting seven numbers *7541888* forever tattooed above his twitching left wrist.

Javier did not receive a very warm welcome. All the influential *Resistance* veteran groups, major labor unions and their parliamentary spokesmen were dominated by the Communists or *PCF*. It, once the largest and best organized individual political party in France. Before the 1980s, when the nation's Left was divided into five mutually-suspicious factions, any single bloc regularly mustering twenty to twenty-five percent of the seats in the National Chamber of Deputies was guaranteed becoming the kingmaker or at least the spoiler of any Left-of-Center coalition government. The leadership of these Marxist veteran groups, labor unions and their representatives in the Chamber also overwhelmingly consisted of people only joining the fight against Hitler after the Soviet Union was invaded on June 22, 1941. Javier, as a centrist, as someone who embraced the struggle while the Moscow-aligned factions still remained neutral, was therefore looked upon by most of his neighbors with immense suspicion if not outright hostility.

Rather than greeted as a hero or praised for his acts of sacrifice, Javier was instead shunned. He was denied all the medals he rightly earned, refused the pension he and his wounded body justly deserved. Never was he invited to ceremonies commemorating the underground's actions. When a monument was erected in the town square listing all those who contributed to the Liberation, Javier's name was left conspicuously absent. Scurrilous stories, often penned by men only joining the *Resistance* after the Allies landed on Normandy, asserting Javier was a collaborator, frequently appeared in the local newspaper. If he lived to a ripe old age and was a successful farmer, Monsieur

Novarro died an angry, embittered man. His deeds of bravery were either demeaned or largely forgotten.

So, what lesson did his daughter take from observing her father's disgraceful treatment? Certainly not opposition to the Left as later events proved. Rather, Juana came to distrust the official leadership of any established institution, secular or religious. She forever looked askance at any set of top dogs purporting to hold sole knowledge of what is correct. She doubted any bureaucracy perceived the truth better than was discovered in this remarkable girl's own searching spirit.

Maria-Miranda Arabaje *RN* first saw the light of day on the southern side of the invisible, meandering national dividing line. As such, she was officially Spanish, although forever insisting herself to be a *Basque*. Seventeen years younger than her husband, Miranda first met Javier Navarro while serving as his nurse during a serious illness he incurred resulting from the warrior's earlier imprisonment at Auschwitz. The pair eventually fell into something approaching love and she became his wife and the mother of their only child. With Javier mainly occupied either managing the farm or confronting his detractors in San Pedro/ St. Pierre, Miranda took up most of the responsibility for raising Juana. Considering the significant age difference between husband and wife, the latter often saw herself as much as her spouse's daughter as his wife. She was therefore Juana's wise big sister no less than parent.

Miranda was never involved as French and Spanish intelligence networks long believed, in terrorist activities. However, she was indeed firmly committed to preserving a distinct Basque culture and to achieving her people's regional autonomy if not necessarily outright independence. Establishing it, *on both sides of the border.* As one result, her daughter became as fluent in Basque as she became in French, Spanish, English, German and Italian. A self-taught sociologist and linguist, Miranda compiled a very large and highly valuable collection of Basque cultural material, one worthy of forming a small museum. Over years of field investigation, she brought together thousands of: tape recordings; personal interviews; films; art works; photographs; old publications; musical instruments; toys; cooking recipes; articles of clothing; weaving and knitting works; household items; and other assorted ethnic paraphernalia—closely documenting her people's ancient, multifaceted heritage. Much of which, Miranda feared, might soon be either lost to time or submerged in Americanized mass-distribution pop existence. Had she lived in contemporary times, Miranda would likely be honored as a famous, perhaps even path-breaking scholar. She'd today be a much sought-after "expert" and celebrated *PBS* talking-head.

A devout, practicing Roman Catholic of mystical persuasion, Miranda, if reluctant to part with her child, nevertheless set up no obstacles to Juana fulfilling the girl's original decision as to how she dedicate her life. Dying before her daughter began achieving full potential, however, Miranda must still have been a little disappointed Juana did not appear as interested as she in promoting Basque studies. Years later, Sister Jeanne sought to make up for what she judged "my act of teenage unconcern for others," for "my terrible adolescent rudeness" by persuading the French Ministry of Culture to purchase her mother's collection and set it up as a museum.

"I might have traveled far" the foundress of The Sisterhood told the television interviewer, "but I never forget the place and the people from whom I came."

BEGINNINGS

....

*A*lthough she traveling across five continents during adulthood, Juana Novarro spent her formative years never far removed from her birthplace in the craggy, snow-capped Pyrenees. San Pedro/St. Pierre with just three hundred inhabitants and its surrounding ancient terraced-farms and fruitful vineyards constituted this girl's entire world until she was seventeen. Yet even in these early sedentary years, the later globetrotter never felt isolated or confined. While limited in geographic scope, her secluded environment nevertheless provided swift entry to all God's kingdom. Reared in such a visually transcendent atmosphere, one, where immediate contact with the Creator, direct union with the unspoiled glory of nature, uninhibited fellowship with medieval saga, were constant intimates, unavoidable daily companions, Juana Navarro like her later companions Mary Preston and Leopoldine Fauré was from her earliest recollections a Roman Catholic of mystical persuasion.

Height
Depth
Width
Near
Far
Light
Darkness
Color

Silence
Melody
Even if one is situated at isolated, too small to appear on a map San Pedro/St. Pierre, a viewer need just gaze about to discover beauty in all its purest, most unadulterated forms. She might contemplate infinite loveliness beckoning from every direction. Born into this fresh, rainbow, dancing, symphonic world, a girl with Juana's yearning soul could not help but feel called upon to devote her life to such a magnificent environment.

"Wow! Super!" the child exclaimed one morning. Long, thick, silky, brown hair covered her face with: high forehead and cheekbones; straight nose; strong chin; piercing gray-green eyes; firm, smooth, soft, tan, Latin color skin. Wearing white bobbysocks, one buckle of her red Maryjanes was come unfastened. "Wow! Super!"

I

"Where has little Juana gone off to now?" asked a worried relative, she come to visit the family from Toulouse. "Is the child well?"

"Oh, yes, Juanita is quite fine" assured her mother wearing a sleeveless green frock, she busy cataloging tape recorded interviews just taken with Basque peasants. "The child is out on the mountain ridge communing with God."

"With . . . *God*?" queried the relative visiting from Toulouse.

"Yes, with God."

"Does the child do this often?"

"Oh yes, indeed, Therese" replied Miranda, with all rightful maternal pride. "My Sweetheart has been chatting with the Almighty nearly daily since she first learned to walk! As she often reminds me from **Psalm 29**-- "*The voice of the Lord is powerful; the voice of the Lord is full of majesty.*""

"It sounds as if the child is planning to become the next Jeanne d'Arc or the new Simone Weil?"

"Ah! The next *Jeanne d'Arc* or the new Simone Weil" reiterated Miranda with a musing smile and romantic twinkle of gray-green eyes."Maybe, my daughter is going to become the next Jeanne d'Arc or the new Simone Weil! This sorry, commercialized world of ours today could certainly do with another *Maid of Orleans* or another *Red Virgin!*"

"Well, just make sure Cherie wears a sweater and hat so she doesn't catch a cold. Make sure too, she doesn't play with matches or decides to starve herself for the sins of others."

II

What do you think God is trying to say to us, today?" Juana questioned a playmate as the two little girls looked across the mountain ledge one cloudless spring afternoon.

"I'm not certain" replied the playmate. "Do you often speak with God?"

"Oh, yes indeed Maria" answered Juana, matter-of-fact. "God and I chat often daily. He decided to appoint me His special chum."

"'Is that so!"

"Now I see! Now I see!" piped Juana with delight. "Now I see what God is trying to tell us! Oh, what a Sweetheart He is, too. He wanted to wait until both we girls got here. Such a gentleman He is! He wanted to wait until both the ladies arrived before speaking!"

She waved graciously across the mountainside.

"Now give Him a wave too, Maria! Go and give Him a wave, too!"

If the Cathars were long departed by the time Juana arrived, the spirit of these Medieval heretics lived on embodied in this girl's belief that we need no clerical intercession to commune with the Almighty.

III

"Is that really, truly what you want me to do next, Lord?" asked Juana, her long, thick, silky, brown hair covering cute face. She, felt much honored to receive this request but also a little unsure as to her ability fulfilling it.

Yes, that was precisely what this unique child was called upon to undertake.

"Could you still possibly grant me just a little time Lord, to prepare?"

If that was best for Cherie, okay. A short time for her to prepare for the mission was granted.

"Thank you, Lord. I pledge to get back to You very soon."

IV

"You were right, Lord!" cried Juana the next morning to her special, otherworldly chum on the cloud-wreathed mountaintop. "You were correct all along Lord! Correct all along, of course! Sorry for me ever even once doubting either Your personal wisdom or Your deep trust in my own ability, in my own courage!"

Juana giggled, looked down embarrassed, her white socks drooped to ankles. She made a meek, anxious circle in the brown pebbled walkway with her red Maryjanes.

"Silly girls like me" the child confessed, "often behave this way—Silly girls like me are frivolous, goofy, weak-minded on occasion." Then, falling on her bare knees, long, thick, silky brown hair again in pretty young face, Juana reached fervently out across the mountain ridge. "Yes Lord! Yes, Lord, I promise! Of course I will obey! Of course I will do as You ask of me! I promise to always be Yours as You wish to always be mine! I will forever be Your warrior! As You guarantee to be forever at my side, I guarantee to be forever at Yours!"

"From this day forth, Lord" shouted Juana, tears of joy running her firm, smooth, unmeddled-with cheeks, "we two are comrades-in-arms! We two are inseparable buddies! Today, tomorrow—and for all ages to come!"

"Bless you Lord! Bless you!" exclaimed Juana when a moment later in seeming reply to the youngster's lifetime's pledge, a soft breeze came down from the peeks to gently caress her bare legs and stroke her panties. The sensation provided the girl not simply a feeling of a greater force's confirmation but also an uncanny, sexual thrill. Not just an ethereal spirit, God was too, Mademoiselle Navarro's lover.

"For it was you who formed me in my inward parts"—she cried, quoting from **Psalm 139**—*"you, who knit me together in my mother's womb. Even before a word is on my tongue, O Lord, you know it completely."*

V

"My little Juana is a most serious, ambitious, very gifted child" observed her mother to their relative visiting from Toulouse. That day, Miranda wore: an open, light pink cardigan; a white dress; white hose and heels, as she checked through the individual reel-shots in a film she just recorded of a Basque wedding. "My little Juana is going to make her family, her clan, and her village so proud—My Juanita is going to put San Pedro on the map—Juanita is going to place our hamlet in the history books! Yes, Juanita will!"

"Mark my word!" declared Miranda sporting a wide satisfied smile on painted lips, she stopping to adjust the angle of her white chapeau. "Just you watch! As the Virgin is my witness! It all makes a Mama feel so good, so satisfied, so fruitful inside! It makes a Mama know she's contributed to the world something unquestionably right and noble!"

VI

Juana demonstrated scant interest as a child in collecting dolls or playing house. If as drawn as any youngster to looking at herself in the mirror and hearing local tittle-tattle, she confided her opinions on such matters not to playmates but to her "comrade-in-arms" atop the cloud-wreathed mountain ridge.

"My Juanita prefers communing with her Special Chum on the mountainside to making a mess of her room, or to whining that Mama hasn't yet bought her daughter the latest ***must have***-toy or the newest fad ribbon!" commented Madame Navarro approvingly. "My Juanita has much better things to do than pestering adults about getting a later bedtime or boasting to her playmates that she owns more things than they which are pink! A most obedient, respectful child, she is."

VII

Adolescence did not change matters. Quite, the reverse. Instead of she devotedly following the activities of narcissist movie stars, sexually-ambiguous *Pop* singers, or athletes with too many muscles to be natural, young teenager Juana preferred navigating the existential. She daily sought to discover exactly how she might fulfill the pledge to her comrade-in-arms atop the cloud-wreathed mountain ridge. If she never immune to periodic inspections of *Vogue* and the other fashion magazines to which Miranda subscribed, her daughter was primarily interesting in mastering the grand scheme of things. *"I press toward the goal for the prize of the upward call of God and Christ Jesus"*– quoted Juana from **Philippians.**

VIII

San Pedro/St. Pierre was too small to possess a library or bookstore of its own. In addition, *FACEBOOK, TWITTER* and *AMAZON* were all yet to be invented. Not discouraged, Juana ordered the publications she wanted from bustling, metropolitan Toulouse. If these coveted packages raveling by regular mail took far longer to arrive, this added wait only served to make their eventual coming more exciting. Almost every afternoon, Juana scampered to the circular red and black metal postbox to look inside and see if the latest order was delivered. Usually, she was disappointed. But finally, when she reached into the cylinder, the long hoped for prize was at last come.

"Ah! The Virgin be praised!" the girl would squeal on these cherished occasions. "The box is here at last!" If denied the conveniences of the *Internet*, she was also spared that system's frequent addictiveness. None of social media's less admirable qualities were present to distract Mademoiselle from the full enjoyment of her latest new books and learned periodicals.

"My Juanita is such a questing, diligent, scholarly child!" commented Miranda in short pattern, sleeveless frock, proudly. "There's nothing my Cherie likes more than a good read! A good think! Why, she's got more brains and spirit than all the boys in this town put-together! My Juanita is going to go far! She will leave her darling, priceless lasting imprint on this world! Just mark my words! As the Virgin is my witness!"

In her quest to discover "how I am supposed-to-do-what-I-am-supposed-to-do," Juana became enthralled with the work of Verlaine, Rimbaud and Claudel. She read and then immediately reread the anthologies she purchased of these poets' verse and plays. So often did she do so, that by the time Juana was just fourteen, her beloved volumes had fallen apart.. Their sacred pages were now only kept together with rubber bands. Luckily, the young admirer already succeed in learning most of Verlaine, Rimbaud and Claudel by heart.

On occasion, Juana declaimed these verses aloud to her comrade on the mountain ridge. This Special Chum was ever eager to listen and to appreciate His little pal's literary knowledge. From Verlaine, the girl finished one famous poem:

> —*Au calme clair de lune triste et beau*
>
> *Qui fait rever les oiseaux dans les arbes*
>
> *Et sangloter d'extase les jets d'eau,*
>
> *Les grands jets d'eau au sveltes parmi les marbes*

Next, from *a* celebrated *R*imbaud piece, she concluded:

> —*Et le poete di qu'eaux rayons des etoiles*
>
> *Tu viens chercher la nuit, les fleurs que tu cuellis*
>
> *Et qu'il a vu sur l' eau. couchée en ses longs voiles,*
>
> *La blanche Ophéila flotter, comme un grand lys*

At last, from Claudel's "La Preface," the girl cited:

—Je sais que tout est fini derriere moi et que le retour est exclu.

Donne avec un profond tressaillement, mon ame, dans ce pays completement inconnu!

Pourquoi tarder plus longtemps sur ce seuiil preparateur?

Viens, si le nom d'un quelque douceur.

IX

"My Juanita is so well-read a child!" said Miranda, today dressed in her immaculate-white nurse's uniform and headdress, stopwatch at right breast, stethoscope around neck. "In addition, Cherie possesses both an exceptional memory and so grand an ability to perceive the deeper meaning of things. She's always been the spiritual sort. Yes, the spiritual, otherworldly sort! Maybe in another time and place, my daughter would upon growing up wish to become a—but I digress."

X

Also winning this unique kid's fascination were the literary and historical articles regularly published in the periodical *Revue des Deux Mondes*. She also took a particular fancy to Giorgio Visari's classic *Lives of the Artists*. These works met the same fate as her anthologies of the three great French poets. So often were they read and then instantly reread, that by the time their owner was just fourteen, her copies of *Revue des Deux Mondes* and Visari were only held together but rubber bands.

"My Juanita never reads her material passively or just once" explained Miranda, she recently promoted to head (or *Mother*) of all the nurses in the Toulouse Central Hospital "No mere bystander is my girl! When it comes to literature, Cherie attacks it! Darling overwhelms it! Why, she's the Napoleon, the Bismarck, the Caesar of letters!"

XI

San Pedro/St. Pierre not being large enough to warrant a school of its own, the village children were five days a week driven in an orange and black bus fifteen kilometers to attend classes at the larger town of San Miguel/St. Michel. The Navarro family (Madame and Mademoiselle in particular), might be devout Roman Catholics but their section of France was since the bitter anti-clerical conflict of the early Twentieth Century, entirely dominated by vehemently-secular politicians and bureaucrats. As a result, Juana, like all the other boys and girls of Ariege Department went to a government school. "Religion" insisted Georges Clemenceau in 1904, after the *Third Republic* severed its Concordat with the Vatican, seized all Church property, and expelled a number of politically-active Catholic orders from the country, "has absolutely no business meddling in public affairs. It must also never be allowed to poison the impressionable minds of our children."

Mademoiselle Navarro soon established herself as the school's star pupil. Each year, she captured prize after academic prize. The girl came out as **Number One** in every succeeding examination. She won this distinction in history and in literature, in essaying-writing, in civics and in geography. Each year she came away as First in her class, as First in the entire Department of Ariege. No other French teenager (of either sex) before or since achieved Juana's level of academic triumph in secondary school. By the conclusion of her first year at the lycée, *Juana Navarro* was become a synonym for *Best Student*.

"Why don't you keep to your studies as Mademoiselle Navarro does?" parents repeatedly scolded their own less academic-minded offspring.

"Why don't you learn from Mademoiselle Navarro's fine example!?

"All those prizes the Little Thing brings home!"

"She's also such a well-behaved young lady!"

"Mademoiselle Navarro must make her parents so proud!"

If such repeated adult hectoring could only guarantee jealousy in the younger generation, bad feeling in the class toward *Smartypants, Teacher's Pet* already existed. Most of this ill-will emerged from the masculine component of the school. As is all too common with girls who are both pretty and very intelligent, who, are both interested in complicated "male" subjects yet tend to view them from a lofty, spiritual, "feminine" perspective, Juana frightened boys. They were at once attracted to her sexually and intimidated by her "unnatural," "non-girl" brain-power. Similar to her later friend Mary Preston, Juana Navarro was considered off-putting, judged as if she belonged to a different, far more aggressive animal species. Being pretty, kind and empathetic brought her no advantage with the *Opposite Sex.*

If on two occasions a boy held Juana's hand, a boy twice kissed her, twice stroked her bare thigh—episodes, she found as stimulating as any normal teenage girl, neither transitory Lochinvar wished to provide Mademoiselle Navarro those lovely, terrific, previously-unknown experiences a third time.

"Most boys aren't brave enough to hold my hand, to kiss or to touch me even once!" observed teenage Juana, sleeveless. Crossing her pretty legs opposite, hem of white dress receding, she was perplexed at her uniquely feminine ability to both swift attract and then as promptly scare away curious male classmates. "If I just cried *Boo*! I bet the boys would likely all run away and hide under their desks."

Save when they peering furtively over this mysterious girl's shoulder in class to discover the correct answers to test questions, or when trying to copy her prize-winning school essays, most boys avoided all unnecessary contact with Juana.

When Mademoiselle Navarro queried the lads about their views on subjects dear to her own heart, they sheepishly confessed to not subscribing to *Revue des Deux Mondes;* they admitted to only skimming the *Iliad,* to never having read Verlaine, Rimbaud and Paul Claudel. As for Visari's *Lives of the Artist,* most chaps were unaware that work even existed.

"And just imagine one day, when I'm older, me actually marrying one of those weaklings!" speculated Juana., again crossing her pretty bare legs opposite, hem of short skirt receding. "Me, allowing myself to become subject to one of these silly characters' every passing whim and momentary fancy! Me, doing all the cooking and cleaning like an unpaid servant! Getting no thanks for my services. Me, feeling obliged to look the other way when my husband goes Tom-catting with dark-roots women half his age. *Yes, darling, yes darling*–I'll be expected to say–*You're the man so you make all the decisions, You must be right, I won't argue. After all, I'm only a stupid woman*--Blah! Me, do all the child-raising and shopping!. Me, compelled to laugh at my husband's bad jokes, to punch-out babies for him nearly every year! Settle his debts. Blah! Ick! Foolishness! Not for me!

"I take my husband's surname!" she scoffed, adjusting her bobbysocks. "Why, my husband ought to take *mine!*"

She thought too of the way Javier spent so much time quarreling with the Communists and the leftist press that he abdicated nearly all responsibility for raising their child to Miranda.

"Papa always forgets my birthday, Mama's too!" recalled their daughter. "On the morning I graduated from lycée, Papa could not come to the ceremony because he was too busy either arguing with one of the veteran's groups or delayed at the newspaper complaining about its latest article about him! Hmmm!"

"Likely, the boys in my class will all turn out just the same way," she guessed."*Sorry, Juana, I'd really love to stay and help out with our kids –I also really mean to get that blasted leaky faucet fixed.. However, I already promised to meet my chums at the club to grumble all day about politics. You're always so dependable, so responsible Cherie. You're the person everyone looks to in a crisis. It's best raising our kids and fixing the leaky faucet be left to you.*"

"No! No!" Juana decided that very afternoon. Despite all evidence to the contrary (those exhilarating gropes to her bare thigh included), "boys are ultimately just a waste of a girl's valuable time. I can break my own individual creative path in life, engrave my own lasting, worthwhile, feminine mark on history. A girl needs no boy's silly, make-me-do-all-the-work while he takes-all-the-credit assistance–thank you very much. I'll plot my own course."

"Besides" thought Juana, "what's a temporary, wandering-eye boyfriend worth compared to the eternal love of God!"

BACHO

....

"*It's* time for you to go to bed now, Cherie!" instructed Miranda, entering her daughter's. book, periodical, chart and map cluttered bedroom.

"Can't I please work just a little longer, Mama?"

"Not unless you wish to receive another well-deserved spanking!"

Juana set down latest volume, looked at her mother worried.

"No, I thought not" commented Miranda with a reassuring smile.

She pecked Juana affectionately on her right cheek, lovingly caressed the girl's mounds of sinuous dark brown locks.

Miranda glanced about at the carpet. Then smiled, relieved.

"From downstairs I could hear Cherie pacing back-and-forth so often, memorizing facts and figures, reciting aloud speeches she intends to deliver, debating with herself. I became concerned that my child might also wear-through the carpet. Luckily, it appears I've arrived just in time."

"Sorry, Mama."

"No worry. Now go and prepare for bed while I put these weighty tomes and learned magazines and large charts in something approaching order.

"Yes, Mama, I'll prepare for bed."

"And don't forget to brush and floss your teeth! Mama doesn't want her famous little scholar to have bad breath or to have a grin which looks like a toothless skull."

As Juana went into the bathroom to brush and floss her teeth, next, change into a nightgown, Miranda sought to make order out of scholastic chaos. She placing the books on the right, the periodicals on the left, the maps inserted in yet a third place.

"I want you do go to bed now Cherie because you must not be drowsy when the examination begins. I want all your cognitive and academic functions to be flowing at their traditional full power.

"Yes, Mama."

"And make sure to say all you prayers to The Virgin."

"I promise."

I

Tomorrow, Juana was to begin her Baccalaureate examination. While no precise equivalent is found in the United States, a Baccalaureate is roughly similar to a Bachelor's Degree from either an *Ivy League* or other top tier private university like Stanford, Johns Hopkins, MIT, the University of Chicago. Except, that a Baccalaureate is obtained at just age 17, 18 rather than at 21, 22 after four additional years of college study. Quite a prestigious achievement in itself, many in France and her overseas possessions feel winning a "Bac" or "Bacho" is impressive enough alone for them to embark on a successful career even without graduating university.

Juana planned to compete for the Liberal Arts or *Littéraire* version of the Baccalaureate. This involved: first, passing tests on: French literature, French history, French Philosophy; French Rhetoric; then: mastering a quiz about current events. One part of the examination involved writing essays; a second part, was oral; a third section, devoted to debate; a fourth, consisting of the applicant delivering impromptu speeches about previously undisclosed subjects offered to him or her by the examiners. Sometimes, the person taking the test worked alone, at other times as member of a small group of fellow students. It was not supposed to be easy. First instituted by Napoleon as a means of training government bureaucrats, the "Bacho" over time became a hallmark of the entire French educational system.

"This year, the Baccalaureate examination is being held for we southerners in Pau" explained Miranda, she wearing: a short, sleeveless white frock; white pantyhose and heels. At the blue *Renault* wheel, her daughter seated just beside, Miranda began negotiating the winding, pebbly brown road leading out of San Pedro/St. Pierre and onto the battleship gray Ariege Department freeway. "Remember my Auntie Maria?"

"Of course I do, Mama. During The War, Auntie Maria recruited and directed her very own underground unit. She carried out a good number of sabotage operations, collected and transmitted valuable intelligence to the Allies in London. She also helped Jews and downed Allied fliers escape into Spain. She was a real big *Resistance* figure. When the Communists betrayed her to the Nazis, she never talked. Women aren't supposed to be brave. Women aren't supposed to be strong under torture. Yet Auntie Marie was. She never broke. I don't know why they never make a movie about her."

"When we arrive though, don't ask her any questions about her experiences in the War" advised Miranda. "Auntie Maria never likes to talk about that subject. Last Spring, some American television company asked to interview her but she politely turned them down. No matter how heroic Auntie Maria was during the The War, raising the subject always gives her the ferocious jitters and later terrible nightmares."

"Yes, Mama. I promise."

The *Renault* sped the Stalin-gray national highway south.

Even in summer, the mountaintops were covered in snow.

"Today Auntie Maria lives in retirement at Pau," continued Miranda. "Since the Bacho examination will be administered over a few days, Auntie Maria offered her spare-bedroom to us. We can sleep there while you take the test. I'm sure you will also enjoy touring Pau. It's a lovely, historic town. It'll also be quite a change from where Cherie has been living until now."

II

"Awesome!" piped and bubbled Juana, she gazing transfixed at the spectacle unfolding outside the *Renault* window. "No! No! *Really* awesome*!*"

"That's just as the reaction I suspected you'd have" commented Miranda with a smile. She, pleased if not surprised by her daughter's reaction upon first casting eyes on–The Big City.

For a girl born and raised almost entirely in isolated mountain villages, Pau, the administrative seat of Pyrénées-Atlantique Department about fifty miles east of the Bay of Biscay, was a memorable experience, indeed. With a central city population of approximately 80,000, it was for someone reared in 300-member San Pedro/St. Pierre, a vast metropolis.

"Wow! Super! Awesome! No! No! *Really* awesome!"

"I see you are quite impressed" observed Miranda, at the wheel, making a left.

Next, a right.

Soon, making another right.

Then, steering directly ahead.

"Awesome!" squealed Juana, transfixed at the view bound the car window. No! No! Re*ally* Awesome!"

"Auntie Maria will be most pleased at your opinion of her town, Cherie."

"Awesome! No! No! *Really* awesome!"

Juana's conclusion is endorsed by more than a few others. With the town's–domed, often cloudless deft blue sky; its high altitude and braising fresh air; viewers offered a stunning panorama in each direction of the snow-capped Pyrenees; houses built in off-white, tan and khaki limestone with black tiled roofs along streets intersected by snaking russet cobblestone streets; sporting graceful beige public squares and yellow-white limestone river-spans; all, surrounded by well preserved outer white circular Medieval walls and donjons—Pau is indeed a lovely, thought-provoking place. One might even call the spot a mini-Paris. The birthplace of Margaret of Angouleme, Jeanne d'Albret and Henry

IV, it was a major site of *Renaissance* intellectual thought. Until the end of the Sixteenth Century Pau was too, the capital of the independent kingdom of Navarre. If Biarritz is a more famous upscale watering hole, Pau became even earlier a beloved destination of upper class British tourists and expatriates. Today, the town prospers as the headquarters of the French space and aeronautics industry.

"Awesome!" reiterated Juana. "No! No! *Really* awesome!"

"This is the child I so often spoke of to you, Auntie Maria" explained Miranda, speaking in Basque, as she and her daughter were greeted warmly at their hostess's three story limestone house at No. 5 Rue Philosophe. Both travelers made scrupulously certain to exit the *Renault* in a manner only proper for ladies wearing a dress. "*Mademoiselle Brains*, everyone calls her back at San Pedro."

"I am so glad we can at last meet, Cherie" pronounced the *Resistance* heroine with delight, her words also spoken in Basque, the numbers *100393* hauntingly tattooed above her left wrist. "I have heard so much about you Sweetheart. Now at last we can sit down and have long chat. I will be so delighted to hear at length and at leisure about all your many scholastic accomplishments."

Juana graciously curtseyed deep.

Smiled humbly.

Fiddled with her short, sleeveless, violet frock.

"So well-behaved a child she is too, Miranda" the hostess complimented her niece. "You've raised her well!" The deep, still very painful wounds Madame Arabaje received from being tortured by the Nazis were invisible under her blue, long-sleeve, closed-necked dress.

"Thank you so much Auntie Maria. I try to be as good a mother as I possibly can. Especially, of a daughter. And a daughter in these current *Pop* music, dark-roots, push-up bra, sex-and-violence movie star times! The Child is my own personal accomplishment. I understand God gave her to me for a reason and not out of mere whim. I keep that fact always in my consciousness."

"I therefore keep The Child on a very short leash," continued her parent. "The Child's learned she'll promptly get a spanking if ever disobeying me. She knows she'll immediately get several good smacks if ever daring to talk back or she getting it into her little head to wear trousers, to try dope, or to come home after dark. I make sure The Child knows to say all her prayers to the Virgin daily, to go regularly to Mass, go to Confession every month."

"Splendid" replied Madame Arabaje, most impressed with her niece's parenting skills. "Splendid."

"I'm concerned for Darling's immortal soul, not just her superb intellect," summarized Miranda. "I hope I've done a good job raising and guiding her. I've done all I can so that The Child is not only a famous scholar but also a faithful Christian. I've seen to it that Cherie is a novel thinker but also one who knows she must respect her elders."

Juana again graciously curtseyed deep.

Smiled humbly.

Fiddled with her short, sleeveless, violet frock.

"I hope I can at least in part match all the hoopla about me, Madame Arabaje." ventured Juana shyly, she too now speaking in Basque.

"Don't fret, Cherie. Your Mama always tells me the truth."

III

Coup in Turkey
Famine in Ethiopia
Civil War in Yugoslavia
Cyclone in India

"Well, here goes" whispered Juana the next morning. With her long, thick, silky, brown hair tied back with a green satin bow, she wearing her school uniform of–monickered navy blue jacket and red tie; white blouse; plaited gray skirt; white bobbysocks; flat, black shoes fastened with buckle at side–the young scholar departed Madame Arabaje's house to take the fateful examination. All her books, ringed-notebooks and pens were loaded into the girl's khaki backpack. "Now it's time, as the Americans say: 'to face the music–'to show I can walk-the-walk as well as talk-the talk.'"

.Stopping for a moment to adjust her socks, Juana conferred again with her Special Chum on the mountain ridge. "Dear God, please give me strength. Dear God, please give me knowledge, wisdom and fortitude. Please, make my success be in your name and be for your glory."

Then after pause:

"Dear God, let me make all those who love me, rightly proud."

Apparently, the Almighty heard the girl's supplication. When the ordeal was at last complete, it proved to be for Juana far more than worth the travail. The essays she wrote on Verlaine, Rimbaud and Claudel are still considered the finest pieces of short nonfiction writing ever authored by a French teenager. In addition, of the more than 800,000 Baccalaureate applicants from across France and its overseas possessions that year, Mademoiselle Navarro's performance was ranked (as would later too that of her future friend Pascale Kedari) in the top 1%.

"Awesome! No, *really* awesome! Thank you so much, God" chirped Juana upon learning the results. "Bless you! Bless you! It's your victory as much as anyone's, God!. I only succeeded because I trusted in you! May I in all things serve as your instrument, serve as your disciple, oh Lord."

In seeming reply to her pledge, a soft breeze come down from the mountain peeks gently caressed Juana's bare legs and stroked her panties. The experience provided her both a higher force's approbation and an uncanny sexual thrill. Not simply an ethereal spirit, God was also Mademoiselle Navarro's lover.

Juana's two relatives were overjoyed by the girl's triumph. They believed their traditional concepts of daughter-rearing were vividly proven the correct ones.

"What a splendid child you've delivered, Miranda!" proclaimed Madame Arabaje. "What a wonderful scholar you've made of this little bookworm! You certainly raised Sweetheart in the right firm, stern but ever-loving way!"

"And just imagine!" replied her niece, bubbling with all rightful maternal pride. "When I was Cherie's age, girls weren't supposed to be educated! *'Girls are supposed to be kept at home'* people advised. *'Putting education into a girl's impressionable little brain only leads to trouble.'* On having a girl of my own though, I thought I mighty just take a chance. I sent her to school anyway. See, the result! Such a studious little mouse, The Child has become.

"Not that I would advise sending girls to school become a regular practice!" swiftly Miranda added, she fearful her own challenge to convention might be misinterpreted. No hippie radical, pot-smoker Miranda! No fear she or her offspring ever be seen wearing trousers! "Permitting daughters not as obedient, God-fearing as mine to venture beyond the home unsupervised usually leads to unfortunate results."

IV

Landslide in Bolivia
Flood in Bangladesh
Massacre in Armenia
Refugee c crisis rocking Africa

No immediate obligations summoning them back to San Pedro/St. Pierre and widowed-Madame Arabaje much pleased with her visitors' company, Miranda and Juana decided extending their stay in Pau for an indefinite time. In the following weeks, the three three ladies visited all the historic sites. They wandered through the Medieval donjons; investigated the Renaissance chateaus; meandered the cobblestone streets; contemplated the thought-provoking public squares and graceful river-spans. The trio ate at noted cafés on distinguished boulevards; enjoyed museums and celebrated homes. Amidst the bracing fresh air, beneath the clear delft blue domed-sky, they spent many minutes gazing at the unforgettable panoramas of the snow-capped Pyrenees. If Juana was yet to visit the nation's capital, Pau served as a nice foretaste.

"See! See! Over *there*" indicated Juana, pointing at a mountain pass in the distance, as the three ladies stood atop a Medieval donjon. "See! See! Over *there*. *That's* where Hannibal led his elephants."

V

Yet the tawdry larger world could not be held at arm's length forever.

"Look Mama, look! See what just came in the mail!" cried Juana running into the living room with the day's newly arrived post in her raised eager right hand.

"Give it to me! Let me see, Cherie" replied Miranda, indicating she now be handed the bundle.

"Yes, Mama."

Miranda thumbed through the letters and packages.

"The diploma has just arrived from the Ministry of National Education" piped Juana. "It must contain the diploma announcing my Baccalaureate."

"So it must!" seconded Madame Arabaje. "So it must! The Child passed in the top 1% of all the applicants. The top 1% of those taking the examination throughout France and all her overseas possessions! More than 800,000 kids this year! We must get this document framed! Then, everyone can see the child's accomplishment in all its glory!"

The large envelope containing the document was quick but studiously opened.

"Wow!" cried Juana. "Awesome! No, *really* awesome!"

Yes, there the manifesto was in all its opulent, so hard-won for splendor.

Printed in fancy antique script on thick parchment; official seal and stamp of the French Fifth Republic at top; it dated; the signatures of the President, the Prime Minister and the Minister of National Education appearing near the bottom—this was a proclamation worthy to be preserved in a place of honor and for its winner to devotedly cherish until her dying day.

Then, as three pair of excited green feminine eyes came to the critical words, a trio of delicate voices gasped in painful disbelief.

The Baccalaureate was awarded not to a girl named Maria-Juana but instead to a boy christened *Juan-Maria*.

"Shit! Flying fuck! Christ!" exclaimed Miranda, in adamant Basque

"Damn-it! Good Lord!" cried Madame Arabaje, in slightly less vehement Basque.

"So much for adults punishing kids for using bad language or for taking The Lord's name in vain" reflected Juana, silently.

"The poor child, the poor child!" collectively opined Miranda and her Auntie. The two adults each held Juana close. They covered her with protective kisses, lovingly caressed the young scholar's thick, silky, long brown hair."The poor child, the poor child! This to happen after the little thing's so strenuous, dedicated labors!"

"Don't worry Cherie" promised Mama, "this frightful oversight will be seen to! "Don't be frightened Darling. This terrible mistake will be swiftly corrected!"

"This is what always happens" added Madame Arabaje, "whenever you let those godless-Socialists meddle in matters that are none of their business!"

"Slimy politicians," cried Mama, "have no right to stick their runny-noses into our children's education!"

"I'll bet you" predicted Madame Arabaje, "that none of those stupid office-seekers ever passed a Baccalaureate."

"At least, not without cheating!" said her niece.

"Yes, certainly, at least not without cheating!

"Dreadful! Dreadful!"

Miranda and her Auntie Maria each held Juana close.

The two adults covered the girl with protective kisses.

The ladies again lovingly caressed the young bookworm's long, thick, silky, brown hair.

"I'm not worried" Juana promised, also speaking in Basque, she more calm and composed than the tearful adults. "It's a terrible pain but it can be easily corrected by mailing this mistaken one back. I know that my name and my record is on the government computer system."

She adding: "two decades ago, before we got into computers, when all these records were just on paper, an error like this one, would take months-and-months-and-months to fix. If even then! Now, however, it will be much speedier."

Juana paused.

"Still, this is terribly annoying."

"Mi! you've raised the child well, Miranda dear" observed Madame Arabaje.

"I hope this isn't a sign of things to come, though" commented her niece, she happy at Juana's show of confidence but also anxious as to whether the printing mistake on the Baccalaureate diploma might possibly be a harbinger of greater ill to come.

"I pray it be so, *too*" reiterated Madame Arabaje, picking up a hairbrush atop nearby table so that she might begin setting in order what Juana's protectors just made the girl's thoroughly-entangled locks.

Brush, brush, brush, brush,

."The Child has worked so long and so hard, so diligently and so determined on her work, The Child certainly deserves respect and recognition for her learned, Christian labors."

Brush, brush, brush, brush

"Ouch!"

"Sorry, Cherie"

Brush, brush, brush, brush–

VI

If the elders were not as *computer-literate, were* less *techno-savvy* as the teenager, Miranda and Madame Arabaje were also more knowledgeable concerning the ways of the paper-pushing, status-conscious, middle-level bureaucracy world. While **Maria-Juana Navarro** and her distinguished academic record was indeed located in the labyrinthine records of the Ministry of National Education, so too, now was a file on the newly created **Juan-Maria Navarro**. A slight typing mistake, one theoretically fast and simple to correct, instead launched a mammoth altercation rumbling its nasty, unforeseen presence throughout all the seldom visited backrooms and little seen byways of French government. No sweet-talking professional office-seeker or paunchy, receding-hairline-bureaucrat (of any political persuasion) wishing to take responsibility for the error, Miranda and Madame Arabaje were considered troublemakers for making the ensconced, self-important clerics embark on serious, unwanted extra work. Solving the problem took many months. Even today, a few significant *I*s need to dotted and *T*s crossed.

> *First, sign this, Mademes*
> *Next, fill-out **this** form.*
> *In triplicate*
> *Mail it **here***
> *Not, **there***
> *Pay **this** amount*
> *Submit two affidavits*
> *No, three copies of the disputes items*
> *Give us sworn statements by the authorities directly in-charge*
> *Make your complaint known to the Ministry of the Interior, as well*
> *And to the Ministry of Youth Affairs*
> *You must understand Mesdemes, issues of this kind take time.*

The following year, Juana at last obtained the precious scroll bearing the corrected words. All the same, this mysterious Juan-Maria Navarro continues to stubbornly linger in French governmental files. His steadfast refusal to disappear poses the young lady many potential mailing address, banking, passport, credit card, career, purchasing and tax difficulties. Today, however, Mademoiselle Juana's chief concerns are found elsewhere.

VII

Time passed

Seasons changed

Leaves in chestnut trees along Rue Philosophe grew more colorful in shade.

"Look at this!" excitedly said Madame Arabaje, speaking in Basque, the latest edition of the Roman Catholic daily, *La Croix*, in her hand. "Look at this Miranda!"

"What do you see, Auntie Maria?" replied her niece, she too in Basque

The two ladies, each in a soft-color patterned dress, were seated side-by-side in blue overstuffed armchairs placed between a reading lamp atop polished oak lowboy with shined brass shelf handles and knitted lace coverlet.

"I just saw that the Minister will be visiting Pau on Friday." explained Madame Arabaje. "He's come to see the students who achieved the top scores in this year's Baccalaureate examination. That naturally includes The Child."

Especially, since The Child won the highest score of all! The highest score achieved in written memory! Boy or girl!"

"What a splendid child, you've born and raised Miranda, dear!"

"I so wish they would stop calling me—*The Child*" muttered Juana, in French, she seated at a nearby writing table, editing her latest composition about Descartes. As on the day of her historic triumph, Juana wore her girls' *Lycée uniform* of: monickered navy blue jacket and red tie; white blouse; plaited gray skirt; white bobbysocks; black flat shoes fastened with buckle at side."I so wish Mama would stop calling me *The Child*—"

SMACK

SMACK

SMACK—on Juana's small, tender fanny.

"There'll be no further disobedience from you, Cherie!" declared Miranda after forthright response to her daughter's grumbling. "As long as my little scholar remains in Mama's care—as long as Cherie lives under Mama's roof—as long as Mama cooks all Cherie's food, buys all Cherie's clothes, pays all her bills and bears responsibility for any trouble her little one might get herself into—Mama has the right to call Cherie whatever Mama wishes!"

SMACK'

SMACK

SMACK—on Juana's small, tender fanny.

Miranda stuck out her tongue at rebellious offspring.

"Yes, Mama" answered Juana acknowledging defeat, she nursing her sore fanny. "Yes Mama. You always have the right to call me whatever you wish."

33

"Good! That's settled, my so well-haves, my so dutiful–*Child*"

"Now, back to your essay on Descartes!" admonished Miranda.

"As you wish, Mama."

"Anyway" continued Madame Arabaje, she furtively casting Juana a comradely smile, "the arrival of the Minister could prove an excellent means to leapfrog over all this bureaucratic nonsense and get the words on The Child's diploma corrected."

"You think so, Auntie Maria?"

"Yes, Miranda dear. My late husband, your Uncle Rodrigo, was quite a local paladin for the Conservative Party. Each time the big shots in Paris needed something done for them down here in the Pyrenees, each time their newest General de Gaulle-wannabe had to be shown the ropes in our neck-of-the-woods, the party leaders in Paris instinctively turned to your uncle Rodrigo. Why, today, were it not for my Rodrigo's expert assistance, this current, fancy-pants *Minister* would be instead just some seasonal farm laborer up to his knees in manure!"

She smiled, thoughtful.

"I believe that after all my family has done for Monsieur Belanger over the years, the very least our *Minister* should do in return is to grant 'Rodrigo's lonely widow" an audience! He, do it for her a minor favor. After all, a photo-op with the likes of me is sure to garner him some additional support in the up-coming parliamentary election! Our party so relies on the *Sweet Little Old Lady*-vote."

VIII

Large, hopeful, restive crowds assembled in Pau's main public square. All members of this swaying throng–women, men; girls, boys; poor, rich; liberals, conservatives; admirers, critics–each, wishing to catch a glimpse, or, if chance might smile, even touch, possibly share a few word with an individual European mass media roundly claimed to be soon the next president of France. As he exited his shiny, black, feline, stretch limousine, sharpshooters in army fatigues appeared on the black tiled mansard roofs of neighboring limestone buildings. At street level, plainclothes security men in dark glasses opened a corridor for Minister Thomas Belanger to travel.

AFP, BBB, Reuters television equipment buzzed.

Paparazzi furiously snapped their cameras.

About 50 meters ahead on the receiving line–Madame Arabaje: in corn color chapeau, blue dress and heels; neutral shade pantyhose; Miranda, in: white chapeau, pantyhose and .heels, light gray, two-piece woman's *Power suit;* Juana: wearing her girl's lycée uniform–waited patiently for The Minister to approach.

"Let me do the talking" advised Madame Arabaje. "The Minister has known me since he was wearing short pants."

"Wait! See! A Basque terrorist!" gestured abruptly one member of the muscular, frowning, dark-glasses wearing security detail to a fellow guard. "*That one?*"

In an instant, Miranda was seized by three brawny plainclothes policemen, shoved into a nearby truck and driven off to parts unknown.

As if nothing occurred, The Minister continued on his royal progress, a forced grin and twinkle on his thin lips and in his needy eyes. Like a Medieval monarch who's semi-divine physical contact was said to cure scrofula, he reached out to permit the undulating tide of well-wishers touch his sacred person.

"Monsieur Belanger! Monsieur Belanger! Remember me" called-out Madame Arabaje. Her niece's arrest was carried out too speedily for Auntie Maria to yet understand what happened. "I'm Madame Arabaje. Remember me! I'm Madame Arabaje! You used to always stay at my rooming-house! Remember on the second floor–at the end of the hall–in the room with the window looking out on the garden!–I used to cook you breakfast, lunch and supper. I used to darn your socks. I played the board game with you–we often talked together about both literature and current events!–I'd please like to speak to you for just a moment when you're free. It's about this little, gifted niece of mine!"

She pointed to deep curtseying Juana found just beside.

The Minister looked into Madame Arabaje's eyes for a split second.

He clearly recognized this pleading woman. He instantly knew of all the earlier events she spoke. He understood without doubt that his entire career, all his worldly success was due entirely to this old lady and her late husband.

"Yet why should I give a damn about that crone now!" the man thought, haughtily. "After all, today I'm The Minister. Soon, I'm going to be president!"

The split second of mutual acknowledgment passed.

The Minister gave no outward sign he recognized this supplicant better than any of the countless others in the seething multitude.

He walked on.

"Today, we are honored to receive a visit from Minster Thomas Belanger" announced Robert Gille, the mayor of Pau and the Gaullist Party representative for Pyrénées-Atlantique Department in the National Chamber of Deputies. He stood atop a dais in the square's center. "Minister Belanger comes here to provide the Paris government's warm approval of the brilliant scores achieved by our local students in the Baccalaureate examination. He is confident each of these gifted boys and girls will go on to a distinguished political, educational or business career. One, which will make all of France proud."

Gille motioned for Juana and a few other uniformed boys and girls to approach.

"Pull up your socks, Sweetheart!" signaled Madame Arabaje to Juana.

Smiling humbly, hair in face, Juana straightened her socks.

Madame Arabaje threw the girl a warm kiss.

"Yes, to honor these gifted boys and girls is the reason I've come all the way from Paris this morning" announced The Minister, providing Juana's fanny a surreptitious *feel*. "I've heard so much about **Mademoiselle Eve Castelnau**'s great performance in the recent Baccalaureate examination. I pledge that when I am elected your president, I and my government will make the French educational system a model to the world. One of my government's chief objectives will be to assure **Mademoiselle Eve Castelnau** is not only properly rewarded for her noble deeds but also serves successfully as the academic model for all the young ladies of her generation.'

AFP, BBC, Reuters revision equipment hummed.

Paparazzi continued at their frantic trade.

An aide whispered into the Minister's ear that it was time he go to his next event.

"Goodbye! Goodbye!" declared The Minister. "Vive la France! The citizens of Pau have given me a wonderful welcome. One, I shall never, ever forget!"

IX

"I'm free at last" growled Miranda, dusting herself off. "This happens practically every time I go to a public event! I wish those stupid cops would finally get it into their cement brains to leave me alone!"

Miranda was finally released from the national police station. Once more, *The Suspected Terrorist* first needed to undergo the humiliating experience of being: stripped; cavity-searched; sprinkled with skin-burning lice disinfectant; her body sprayed with freezing water jetting from a high-pressure hose; her citizenship questioned; she threatened with deportation; she fingerprinted; photographed; paraded naked through a witness-line; interviewed by unfriendly border guards eager to assume the worst in any seeming-dubious words the prisoner uttered. Then, after she been groped by all her hornie, middle aged, receding-hairline captors, was left for several days in a dark, cold, damp, smelly, vermin-infested cell. All her possessions, along with Madame Arabaje's house, were also summarily rummaged-through and brutally sacked.

As on all previous occasions, no apologies from either the federal cops or the local authorities were forthcoming. Instead, Miranda received simply the traditional suggestion: "Get out of town girlie-troublemaker. And don't come back without first giving us ample notice." This, soon followed the customary: "You've got great legs, a nice ass and terrific boobs too, Sweetie."

"*Intelligence* services!" Miranda growled, observing that not all the money originally in her purse had been returned."The idiots! Little boys playing soldier! Put a couple chevrons on a man's sleeve and he instantly stinks he's become Napoleon! I hope they never treat The Child in this same manner, one day!"

"Just because I wish to document and celebrate my culture" continued the self-taught sociologist, amateur film-director, "doesn't mean I necessarily also want to be a bomb-thrower! Intelligence services! Rubbish! A better term for them is *Unintelligence* services!"

Dedicated throughout her teenage and adult life to lovingly collecting and preserving the elements of her often all-too vanishing Basque heritage, Miranda needed to near-constantly contend with accusations of being directly or in-directly involved with terrorism. Even with charges, of being an assassin, herself! Once, she considered actually moving with her daughter either to Britain, Italy or Germany where the condition for Basques was more amenable. "But" Miranda finally decided, "I'm not going to let those bastards drive me out! Hell, if I do move, then I'll simply be playing their game, doing what they want me to do."

She paused.

"Anyway, my people have actually been living in France longer than the French!"

Glancing at her watch, remembering it was Sunday, Miranda sped back to No. 5 Rue Philisophe. Taking a vigorous bath and hair wash, applying new makeup and perfume, changing into new clothes, she then hurried to join Juana and Madame Arabaje at Mass.

By the time Miranda, now wearing a light gray *Power Suit,* white blouse with black ribbon at neck, neutral-shade pantyhose, black heels and corn-shade chapeau, arrived at *Gothic* St, Jean Church with its vaulting spires and flying buttresses, the service was just concluded. Yves Gautier, the new Bishop of Pau, fond of regularly touring his diocese, stood dressed in colorful regalia atop the main portal's burgundy-shade steps. He, was chatting with the exiting parishioners.

"You possess such a kind, gifted and ever-so thoughtful child, Madame Navarro" complimented Bishop Gautier. "Mademoiselle Juana is a really penetrating thinker! I'm sure that under different circumstances, she would be a noted philosopher. I speak not at all in jest, Madame Navarro. As on each occasion Mademoiselle Juana and

I meet following Mass, we soon become engaged in the most weighty and memorable conversations!"

"I'm most grateful for your high opinion of Cherie, Your Grace" replied Miranda, she both honored to receive the comment about her daughter and also worried the cerebral Dear might be taking up the great man's time. "I only hope The Child is not diverting you from all your critical obligations."

Miranda curtseyed deep

"Oh not at all, Madame Navarro!" assured Bishop Gautier. "I enjoy few things more than discussing the meaning-of-life with your delightful, learned daughter."

Miranda curtseyed deep

This day, Juana wore: a soft pink dress; white bobbysocks; soft pink heels. A white chapeau sat atop the lovely girl's flowing silky brown main. Her hands were in soft pink gloves. Around her left shoulder, she carried sported a white leather handbag.

"Mademoiselle Juana was telling me about how much she wishes to provide recompense to the country and to the world she believes has so freely aided her" recounted Bishop Gautier. "I told her that if this is truly her wish, she ought to extend her education as far as she can. Then, when Mademoiselle Juana becomes a distinguished scholar—as I possess no doubt she will—she can then use her position and influence to bring attention to her village, to aid the studies and talents of the other less famous boys and girls of her birthplace,"

"That" said Bishop Gautier,"will certainly be fine recompense."

"However" he added, "Mademoiselle Juana insists she wishes to do more. She wishes, as she told me 'to give of myself,' to 'give myself to a higher cause.' I replied that if this is truly her wish, I shall do all that my office provides, to assist the Dear."

"And what precisely does The Child have in mind, Your Grace?" asked Miranda.

"Mademoiselle Juana told me that she is yet to fully decide" replied Bishop Gautier. "Mademoiselle Juana tells me that she expects to reach her decision by the time you two pretty ladies return home in a few weeks."

LIKE A DOVE

....

That autumn, following mother and daughter's return to San Pedro/St. Pierre in the wake of the latter's celebrated triumph in the Baccalaureate examination, Juana announced that she had decided to become a nun.

"Has someone talked you into this, Juanita, sweetness?" asked Miranda, anxious, she remembering her daughter's earlier conversation with Bishop Gautier. "His Grace may be a wonderful human being. He may be someone who sincerely wishes to achieve happiness for all humanity. Yet His Grace's knowledge about raising adolescents, especially girls, is quite limited. Taking the veil is also not as simple it appears on television or in the movies."

"No, Mama" replied Juana, guessing her mother's concern. "My decision has nothing to do with my recent chats in Pau with Bishop Gautier. I'm also fully aware becoming a nun is not the same as in the movies"

"Are you absolutely sure–about this, Juanita?" pursued Miranda, halting in mid-sentence to relieve a persistent, hacking cough she recently developed.

":Yes, Mama"

"You've thought about this for a long time?"

"Yes, Mama. I've been thinking about this for a very long time.""

"You sincerely believe you possess a *Calling*?"

"Yes, I do Mama."

40

"This isn't just some kind of teenage girl *phase?* I myself went through this very same kind of teenage girl *phase.* My brother Alfonso: first wanted to be a doctor; then, he wanted to become a lawyer; then, a railroad engineer; still later: a sea captain, a balloonist, a frogman; a parachutist; a pilot, an artist, an astronaut, a spy, a Rock Star, a Communist. Oh! My Lord, you should have seen how upset your Grandmother became when she heard Alfonso wanted to be an atheistic Communist!"

"Girls" continued Miranda, "with far fewer options permitted us in our conservative background, usually go through wanting to be a nurse, a grammar school teacher, or a nun. I eventually became a registered nurse in Toulouse. That's how I met Papa and later gave birth to you."

"And a brilliant nurse you are, Mama!" insisted her daughter. "You're an excellent nurse if there ever was one!"

"So, are you truly sure Juanita this current business is not just a normal girl *phase?*" repeated Miranda, parent still to be thoroughly convinced. "Are you sure this is not the same *phase* Mama went through herself at your age?"

"No, Mama, this is not just a *phase.* I sincerely understand I possess a religious *Calling.* In fact, this realization has been steadily building up inside me since I was little. Repeatedly, I tried to disprove it in my mind with writings and debates and actions. Instead, the more I tried rejecting the truth God sent me, the more often and the stronger I came to accept God's will for me. Yes, Mama, I do indeed possess a religious *Calling,* a spiritual *Vocation.*"

"You're not wishing to join one of those crazy American cults, are you? One, where the members: either: commit polygamy; take dope; hold up signs to cameras at baseball games reading **John 3:16**; run around naked; make fools of themselves in Greenwich Village chanting 'Hare Krishna'–then burn themselves up in Texas or drink poison *Coolaid* in the jungle?"

"No, Mama, certainly not"

"Good! I'm much relieved"

"Still, this is not a decision to be taken lightly, Sweetheart" admonished Miranda, she again halting because of a hacking cough.

"Remember, becoming a nun is not something that Sweetheart can easily get out of. It's not like Catholic Summer camp in Brittany. Nor, should it ever be! If God is actually summoning you to be His bride, you have no choice but to accept. You have no choice but to love, honor and obey Him. Now and forever more."

Then after pausing: "So you are absolutely sure this is the path Darling wishes to take with her young life?"

"Yes, it is Mama. I've prayed and prayed and prayed over it. Each time, God sends me the same answer. Please grant me your permission and your blessing."

Miranda contemplated
A silent minute passing
Then, a second
Third.

"Let Mama think about this for a week" said Miranda. "In the meantime, Child, keep to your studies and don't speak further to anyone on this issue. Mama promises to announce her decision in a week."

She paused.

Then, she commented laconic: "If God has actually won you, He should be prepared to wait at least a week before taking His prize."

Seven days went by.

"Very well" announced Miranda at last. "I knew that your Special Chum on the mountain ridge gave you to me for a reason. I understood He allowed me to possess you only temporarily. I always suspected it was my job to prepare you for an exceptional mission, Now, I see what that exceptional mission is."

Since this is truly God's will "said Miranda, "who am I to stand in the way! I've done my work. Now, it's up to you. I grant you my permission and my blessing. I know Cherie will make her Mama and the world immensely and rightly proud."

I

The fateful morning at last arrived.

Mother Marie de Valois, leader of historic St. Elisabeth's Convent in Hautes-Pyrénées Department, was initially dubious about accepting a seventeen-year-old into her custody. "What if this girl is only going through an adolescent *phase*?" queried the abbess, herself at age just twenty-six, the youngest Superior in the Benedictine Order's fifteen hundred year history. "Yes, yes, it's correct. St. Therese of Lisieux was only fifteen when she entered the Carmelites in Normandy. Yes, yes, it's true, I entered this convent too when I was only sixteen. But remember, St. Therese lived before television and as for me, well, my family left me little choice in the matter. I suspect this new girl was raised in a far less restricted environment. I also bet her parents allow her to watch too many romantic movies. Becoming a nun is a far more complicated undertaking than she sees with Ingrid Bergman, Deborah Kerr, or Audrey Hepburn."

Yet as he promised Juana, Bishop Gautier at last prevailed upon the noble dame to grant permission. He, explaining that: "I personally interviewed Mademoiselle Navarro and can guarantee this remarkable Dear is like yourself, Abbess, both spiritual and wise far beyond her tender years. In today's Americanized, self-absorbed, **Me** era, the sisters of St. Benedict ought to consider it a profound blessing to find this Child among them."

"Besides" Bishop Gautier laughed sly, "assisting the most distinguished student in the entire anti-clerical Pyrenees to take the veil will be a terrific way of sticking-it to the Communists!"

Juana awoke following a night of much tossing-and-turning, hours of unsettling anxiety dreams. The black and white plastic battery clock to her left, registered **6:30 AM.** The girl remained under the sumptuous covers for an additional thirty minutes. It was best to savor this experience as long as possible. After all, she would likely never again lie in this particular warm, comforting bed.

Upon she at last arising, Juana in nightgown, barefoot, her sea of silky brown hair fallen almost to waist, walked over to the French window to catch what might be a last glimpse of Roncevalles/ Ronceveaux Pass. "Ah, such a splendid view!" she mused. "Hannibal, Trajan, Charlemagne, Blanche of Castile, St. Teresa of Avila, Napoleon, Goya, Arthur Koestler, Earnest Hemingway, Simone Weil all, each, once journeyed that way. Perhaps I'll never look out on this vista again."

Seated once more atop her bed, Juana surveyed the framed studio photographs on the opposite papered wall. Verlaine; Rimbaud; Paul Claudel; the latter's tragic sister: Camille, she destroyed by the misogynist *Napoleonic Code* which refused to accept women might posses genius too—all looked across at the idealistic teenager. Each image, provided the youngster preparing to embark on her spiritual journey an enigmatic look of both encouragement and skepticism. Unable to take the photos with her, Juana originally intended contributing them to her lycée. However, Mama had been crying so long and often lately about: "God taking away my precious only baby" that Daughter decided leaving these 8-by-10 glossies with Mama as a keepsake.

Cough, cough, cough, cough, painful hacking cough

As the plastic clock registered **7:30 AM**, Miranda entered Juana's bedroom. Her mother wore: an open, light pink cardigan; a short patterned blue dress; neutral shade pantyhose; white high heals. Two strings of natural pearls gracefully encircled a slender neck. Atop her head with shoulder-length black hair and gold earrings, was a wide, corn-color, Edwardian chapeau. While parent was no longer crying, her eyes were painfully red and bleary. Deep sniffles and smudged makeup further testified to recent sobbing. A protective but also resigned expression was exhibited on Mama's pretty, Latin, mid-thirties, ladylike countenance.

"If you must leave me" said Miranda, holding back tears, "let San Pedro see you this last time in your full loveliness."

Cough, cough, cough, cough, painful hacking cough

After she thoroughly brushed Juana's long, thick, silky brown hair, painted the youngster's face, placed one of her own strings of natural pearls around offspring's slender neck, Miranda proceeded to clothe the girl in the same gauzy, expansive, white wedding dress and veil Mama wore at her wedding to Javier. Finally, Miranda put a fresh, colorful, sweet-smelling corsage in Juana's white gloved hands.

"Remember, the Bridegroom approaches. I wish you to be at your loveliest.

Detecting Juana's concern for Mama's health and a sense of guilt which might still temp the girl to abandon her coming journey, Miranda swiftly intervened.

"Don't worry, Child. The Bridegroom is calling. Knowing He has chosen you as His spouse will be far more than enough to keep me well and thankful."

Over the next four hours, Miranda escorted her daughter dressed as if it were the girl's wedding day, to visit many of the houses in the village. All the important and not so important ladies of San Pedro/St. Pierre were eager to play a role in what was for this isolated mountainside habitation the most memorable occasion in quite some time.

As Bishop Gautier accurately predicted to Mother Marie, the Baccalaureate-winner's decision to "take-the-veil," to "give-up-the-world," intensely annoyed the regional Communist Party. The talented girl's choice deeply offended the local *Resistance* veteran clubs, much angered the Department's rigid anti-clerical faction. "Such professional troublemakers only happy when they're unhappy" being all male, their deeply religious grannies, mothers, wives, aunts, daughters, sisters, nieces and girlfriends were uniformly delighted with the path Juana chose.

"Awesome!"

"Unforgettable!"

"It seems right out of a romantic novel!"

"Or, a Medieval saga!"

"Just as in one of those *three-hankie* women's movies!"

For a brief time, the Navarros were the most popular and widely admired family in the entire region. This festival undertaken more to reward Madame for her pious mothering than to celebrate Mademoiselle's embrace of a religious life, Juana knew she must let Mama enjoy all the well-earned glory. Throughout the occasion, Daughter remained humble, silent, obedient, her eyes demure, as all the village matron's compliments were directed to Miranda.

"What a dedicated, God-fearing mother you are, Madame Navarro!

"You must be ever so proud of The Child, Madame Navarro!"

"This must be a great day for you, Madame Navarro!"

"We all know The Child will so honor our village, Madame Navarro!!"

"We know The Child will be the ideal nun, Madame Navarro! It's so beautiful!"

"It must be terrific knowing you'll be the mother of a saint, Madame Navarro!""

"I promise I won't leave my husband a moment's peace until he agrees to display this splendid event prominently in his newspaper, Madame Navarro!"

"That's a dreadful cough you've got, Madame Navarro! Would you and the precious child like to stay for a cup of tea? Tea will certainly help your sore throat and cough, Madame Navarro."

After this ritual was complete, Juana, dressed in a long silk bridal gown and gauzy veil, white gloved hands clutching a large rose corsage, accompanied by her parents, set off with the rest of the village women just behind. A long, snaking line of newly polished *Citroens*, *Renaults*, and *Peugots* traveled to sprawling, historic St. Elisabeth Convent to attend the pensive seventeen-year-old's formal induction into the Benedictine Order.

"Stop blubbering, Mandy!" snapped Javier at the wheel, to his weeping wife "Our child needs her Mama to be strong for her at a moment like this!"

"I'll try, Javier. I'll try my best," replied Miranda, fighting back tears.

Cough, cough, cough, cough, additional painful hacking cough

Upon reaching their destination, the members of this caravan, all wearing their Sunday Best, climbed out of their cars, each female participant sure to exit her vehicle as ladies should. Next, they all filed into the community's front public church with its 40 meter *Gothic* vault and *Arabesque* flooring, to observe the ceremony. *Byzantine*,

Romanesque, Moor, Gothic, Baroque, Georgian, Neoclassical, Restoration in its centuries-long construction, many contemporary art critics consider this edifice simply a vast hodgepodge of conflicting and sometimes incoherent architectural and painting styles. At the same time, St. Elisabeth's possesses many pieces of priceless art, all of them untouched by the vandalism suffered by so many other religious institutions in 1789. Founded by the sainted-sister of an early-Merovingian king, this convent also serves as a strong, vivid testament to the deep and largely unbroken roots of Roman Catholicism in both French history and culture.

Following an interlude of communal prayer in the public area to the sound of lovely hymns sung by a chorus of nuns invisible behind a steel grille, Juana was briskly escorted away alone by Mother Marie and her chief assistant Sister Francoise.

"Now it's time you come with us girl!" said the young abbess with a sigh and in a stern, reluctant voice. She took Juana firmly by her right arm. "His Grace, the Bishop of Pau informs me that I've now no choice but to accept you. I pray His Grace is not mistaken about your deep faith and about your sincere sense of *Vocation*. So, come come this way."

"Yes, come with us" instructed Sister Francoise, also with a sigh and in firm, resigned voice.

The abbess and Sister Francoise, each aged twenty-six and wearing long black habits and white wimples, each with an ivory-shade *Crucifix* and *Rosary* at her narrow waist, led the young newcomer into an ornate Seventeenth Century *Marian* side chapel. Above the marble, gold and silver altar sculpted by Bernini, was a colorful, busy image of the Virgin ascending to Heaven painted by Rubens.

Here, Juana was swiftly stripped of all her finery.

Next, she stood silent, passive, eyes to the floor, as much of her long, thick, silky brown hair was speedily clipped off.

Finally, she let herself be clothed in a homespun white novice's habit and her now cropped head be covered in a wimple.

"Damn it! This is just like the Dark Ages" whispered one nonreligious guest to another. "It's like The Dark Ages! Lord and servant, baron and serf–They could at least have left the poor Dear's beautiful long hair, alone!"

"Hush up!" whispered friend. "The girl's hair will grow back! Even thicker, too!"

"If you say so. Still, I think this ceremony is barbaric."

"Hush up! The child is not resisting. It's her choice to enter that kind of life."

"If you say so."

"Doesn't she appear lovely!" pronounced a more spiritual lady nearby as Juana, her short hair making her look like a delicate boy, was escorted back to the marble altar, She, now dressed to assume her new role.

"The Dear is going to be a saint!" cooed a second pious matron.

"Cherie will make us all proud!" piped a third.

"So indeed, she will!" concurred a fourth.

"A saint" exclaimed fifth.

The Bishop of Pau, serving as master of ceremonies, then began to speak. His homily was based on the episode in **Mark** recording–*"And just as he was coming out of the water, he saw he the heavens torn apart and the Spirit descending like a dove."*

Miranda's pained voice broke the others chain of thought.

Cough, cough, cough, cough, wheezing Mama's bitter cough

Echo

Echo

"Messieurs and Mesdames, this blessed child–"resumed the Bishop.

Cough, cough, cough, cough, Mama's wheezing bitter cough

Echo

Echo

"I'm taking these things as if they were candy!" whispered Mama to Javier as she gulped down additional headache pills.

"Today, this blessed child is being accepted into–"

Cough, cough, cough, cough, wheezing cough

Miranda now rose to her feet and scampered out, she blushing with deep embarrassment.

Click, click, click, click, click–of high heels on granite resonated far.

In another time and place, this situation might be amusing.

However, this was not another time and place.

At the conclusion of the service, Abbess Marie and Sister Francoise took Juana off with them into the Medieval cloister situated behind a thick, heavy, elaborately carved Seventeenth Century *Baroque* gate.

Javier remained behind in the church after Miranda fled. His emotions long ago exhausted from quarreling with the Communists and the left wing local newspapers, Monsieur Navarro possessed no sentiment left to devote to his only child. In addition, he was annoyed by his wife's recent outburst. As Juana departed into the cloister, Javier offered her only a set of traditional words of pious encouragement and advice. He asked his daughter: "to pray for Papa, for Mama, for your family and for your former town."

"Yes, Papa, I promise" Juana responded dutifully. "I promise to make all my relatives, friends and neighbors justly proud."

"Don't worry. Papa know his little girl will do her very best."

Soon, Javier and only offspring parted, shedding no tears. They, never once looking back to catch a last glimpse of a person, each assumed would never be seen, heard or touched again.

Behind thick, brown *Moor* and *Romanesque* granite outer battlements; amid pensive, winding, uniform-columned black and off-white, horseshoed Alhambra quadrangles; within cool, lovely Cordoba enclosed herbal gardens, their bubbling fountains, arching walls and apple-shaped ceilings decorated with ivory mosaic, gold, red, and lapis-lazuli stucco quotations from the Torah—once a Mosque, the convent was previous still, a synagogue—Juana, first as a novice, later as a full member of this ancient contemplative female religious Order was expected spending the remainder of her life. Entering when only seventeen, she might reside here for a considerable time.

Out-of-sight and now too increasingly out-of-mind, the name *Maria-Juana Navarro* was, save by her loved-ones, heard less in San Pedro/St. Pierre. It, was pronounced not in the streets, not at Mass, nor even by the boy students at her former school, they once so often looking over the girl's shoulder at test time to find the right answer. For those beyond her convent, she became a mere living-ghost. One, who with each passing year grew a steadily vaguer, easier forgotten memory. Yet such was not always to be.

FROM BEHIND THE GRILLE

....

"*How* are you managing so far, my Cherie?" asked Madame Navarro *RN*, dressed in gray *Power Suite,* a black chapeau and long silk veil, white stockings, black heels. A large brass Crucifix was around her slender neck. Seated in the convent's visitors parlor, she was invisible to her listener on the other side of an iron grille. Even though it was a long drive, one demanding an extra fill-up of petrol, Miranda nevertheless traveled to the convent almost weekly to speak to her daughter. Today, was the sixteenth consecutive time the extended journey was made. As sure as she was in believing it a duty to surrender her sole offspring to God, Mama felt no less the intense maternal yearning to hold that only child close. "How are you, my Cherie?"

She stretched her hands through the opening to clutch her daughter's arms tight.

"I am doing very well, Mama" replied her daughter. The girl was now and forever after known as Sister Jeanne. "I could tell from the moment I came here that I made the right decision. This, is clearly where God intends me."

"Please excuse Mama" apologized Miranda, "but I can't get rid of this terrible dry cough. My head also keeps throbbing."

Parent broke into a long fearsome cough.

Her hands temporarily surrendered her child's arm so that they might rest on own painfully throbbing head.

"I so much appreciate your visits and your worry about me, Mama" replied Sister Jeanne with deep anxiety. "But I also don't want you to overexert yourself.

"Don't trouble your blessed little brain about me" insisted Miranda, once more taking her daughter's arms tight. "I know that with your sweet thoughts and prayers, undeserving Mama will make it through."

"I hope so, Mama."

Parent broke into another nasty dry cough.

"But enough about me!" insisted Miranda eagerly, several moments later. "Look what I brought as presents for you and the other good sisters."

She pressed several bags of fruit through the opening, mainly apples, grapes and oranges. All, were firm, smooth, lovely to behold, delicious to taste.

"I know that you *Good Sisters* grow their own food" explained Miranda. "Self-support is after all a major tenet of your Order. The Benedictine are the very first organized communal Catholic Order and date back almost to the time of the Romans."

She paused..

"See. My Cherie! Aren't you proud of Mama? She read up all about you sisters and your *Rule*."

"Yes, Mama. I'm most impressed with your study" replied her daughter from behind the grille.

"Anyway" resumed Miranda, "as a mother, I still can't help but worry if you girls–I mean *sisters*–are eating right. So, before I left home to come here today, I made sure to pack up some boxes of apples and oranges which your father produces on the farm. Eating this fruit will assure that you and the sisters are obtaining your proper amount of Vitamin C."

"Bless you Mama. I know the sisters will greatly appreciate your gift. Of course, you didn't at all need to do it."

"I know I didn't *need to*" answered Miranda," but it makes a mother feel so good doing so."

She shuffled in chair.

Crossed her pretty legs, opposite.

"I also brought a lot of fish which your father caught in our river, my Cherie. I left the catch at the front gate with Sister Francoise. She appears to be you girls' quartermaster—quarte*r mistress."*

Miranda giggled conspiratorially.

":Interestingly enough" she whispered, "fish is actually far more nutritious than beef! If you really wanted to 'do-without' on Fridays, you ought to forsake fish for beef!"

"You're right of course, Mama. But who are we to overturn nearly two thousand years of tradition!"

After first trying to suppress it, the pair exploded into schoolgirl titters.

Miranda then pushed a final gift through the opening in the grille.

"Old buildings like this one must get a terrible draught in the winter, my Cherie. I therefore knitted you these special wool socks. I want you to wear them at night."

"I'm most grateful" replied Sister Jeanne. "I promise to wear them at night. But let me assure you Mama, Mother Marie is insistent the heat goes on in the winter.

A bell rang.

The sound echoed down the winding corridors.

"I've got to go now, Mama" pleaded Sister Jeanne. "The bell means that it is time for communal prayers."

"I understand Sweetheart" guaranteed Miranda, rising to her feet. "I've no intention of diverting you from your Godly duties."

Before leaving, she had one last thing to say.

"My Cherie?"

"Yes, Mama"

"I punished you a lot when you were a child. I often put you over my knee. Yet each time I punished you, each time I put you over my knee, I did so only for your own good. Because, Mama loves you."

"Yes, Mama. I understand. I realize now that each time you punished me, each time you put me over your knee, it was only for my own good. Because, you love me"

"Bless you my darling!" cried Miranda. "Bless you!"

She pressed forward, her arms outspread as if to embrace and to kiss her daughter, Only, to discover the physical barrier between them made this impossible.

I

A week passed.

"Well, Cherie, just as Mama promised, here she is again!" announced Miranda, this time, dressed in well-ironed, immaculate-white old fashion nurse's uniform. A stethoscope around her neck, stop-watch at her right breast, a badge at her left indicated she was now *Mother*–or leader–of the entire nursing staff at Toulouse General Hospital.

Once more, parent reached through the opening in the iron grille to hold daughter's arms tight. "There's nothing I look forward to more than . . . being with my child."

She started to say *seeing my child* but then realized such a wish impossible.

Miranda pressed her offspring's arms again tight.

"Thank you so much for coming, dearest Mama" responded Sister Jeanne. If human hair once clipped, grows back thicker at approximately six inches a year,.this novice's locks, who's cutting caused one observer to cry out in horror, were now expanded into a mop entirely covering the girl's forehead, ears and much of her neck. "I so enjoy it when we get to speak."

"And I too!" answered Miranda with all maternal ardor.

She next opened her purse and removed from it a letter received that morning.

"I've been in correspondence with His Grace, the Bishop, Sweetheart."

"Yes?"

"While delighted with learning you possess a religious *Calling*, His Grace, the Bishop is still very preoccupied with the advancement of your education. Your score at the Baccalaureate examination is the highest ever received in this region *Ever*! His Grace the Bishop does not want that score of yours going for naught."

Miranda rustled in her seat.

Crossed her legs in white stockings, opposite.

"Bishop Gautier" she continued with mounting enthusiasm, "arranged for my Sweetheart to proceed with her studies here at the convent and to eventually obtain a degree from the University of Paris. Doing so by mail. Isn't that marvelous, terrific news, Darling? His Grace did not speak idly when he told us he wishes you to set an example for your generation and region."

"Are you sure, Mama?"

"Quite so, my Cherie! Quite so!"

Miranda shuffled again in her seat.

Crossed her legs in white stockings, opposite.

Adjusted her skirt.

Once more opening her purse, Miranda now removed a set of application papers.

She then slipped the forms through the opening in the grille along with a pen.

"All my Cherie needs to do is sign *these* where Mama wrote **X**, obtain your abbess's permission and then, the process can begin. Mama's little scholar will then be off to the academic races!'""

"I'm quite confident that Abbess Marie will consent" assured Sister Jeanne, signing the application papers with a flourish."Abbess Marie is a most forward-looking, reform-minded lady. I might almost call Abbess Marie a Feminist."

"Lord in Heaven! A Feminist! Does she also wear trousers?"

"I said *almost* a Feminist. And no Mama. Abbess Marie doesn't wear trousers."

"Good. Good. I don't want my only child to be placed under the supervision of crazy socialists."

"As I said before" continued Sister Jeanne, adjusting her habit,"I know Abbess Marie will give her permission for me to study for a University of Paris degree."

"Wonderful! Wonderful!"answered Miranda. "You will become the first in either the Navarro or the Arabaje family to ever win a university degree!"

She mused.

"Just imagine" Miranda reflected at last. "God gave me not only a noble child but a noble child who is also a brilliant academic! What more can a Mama ask for! His Grace the Bishop was correct. Sweetheart is going to make herself a splendid Christian example to all who come after her!"

Sister Jeanne blushed crimson.

The bell announcing time for communal prayer sounded again.

Mother and daughter on either side of the iron grille rose to feet.

Miranda swallowed three more painkillers for her head.

"I must go now, Dear" she said. "Please promise to pray not just for me but also for your father. He may not be the expressive type but I know that down deep he loves you and is proud of you just as much as I. After all that Papa went through during *The War,* it's hard for him to open up and say how he sincerely feels."

"I promise, Mama. I understand Papa loves me too. I promise to pray for him."

"See you next week.

Miranda once more reached forward as if to kiss and embrace her daughter. Only, to again discover the physical barrier separating the two made contact impossible.

II

Three days later, Miranda suffered a brain aneurism. Transported by helicopter to her hospital in Toulouse, she lingered on as a vegetable for a month before mercifully breathing her last. Although Miranda's medical condition had been worsening for some time, Sister Jeanne could not help but feel a deep sense of personal responsibility. She, in a biting, never departing way fearing her decision to become a nun was somehow the ultimate cause of parent's collapse. She therefore arranged for Miranda to be buried on the convent grounds. The place chosen for Mama's final resting place is in a shaded, thoughtful garden beneath an evergreen tree.

In ancient Chinese culture, parents are often ennobled for creating famous children. Miranda Arabaje Navarro was definitely worthy to receive such an honor.

THE STONE WHICH
THE BUILDERS REJECTED

For a decade before this story opens, ancient, historic St. Elisabeth's Benedictine Convent had been wisely governed first indirectly and during more recent years in official fashion by Mother Marie, she christened: Marie-Therese-Adrienne-Michele de Valois-Martignac and her closest friend since childhood: Sister Francoise, before taking the veil: Marie-Therese-Gabrielle-Francoise de Rousillon-Beaufort. Were it permitted, Mother Marie would make her soulmate Co-Abbess. Creation of such a position forbidden in this Order of contemplative nuns, she instead appointed her friend sub-abbess.

If both young ladies possessed many other fine personal qualities, the pair first captured an observer's attention through they being each strikingly attractive. Their lofty, aristocratic character; their graceful, queen-like comportment; long, flowing black habits—served to yet further magnify the duo's exceptional physical beauty. Often, Mother Marie and Sister Francoise exercised their authority over lesser mortals simply through offering teasing, brief physical contact. Soon, *The Two Lovelies* withdrawing once more to their original pedestals. All the other nuns in the convent were desperately in love with them. Admirers considering an encouraging word, a gentle smile, or a soft touch granted by their leaders as something to be cherished more than the greatest of diamonds. In short, Mother Marie and Sister Francoise each possessed like Napoleon, Gladstone, Roosevelt and Nelson Mandela, that magical, mystical, it as invisible as it too. so apparent to behold attribute called: *Presence.*

Sister Jeanne, also quite pretty, was not immune to this otherworldly charm. The day she sought permission to obtain a University of Paris degree by post, Miranda's daughter fell on her knees before the abbess. The teenager's hands were clasped in supplication, her watery green adolescent eyes pleading.

"Oh, but of course you may, Cherie!" replied Mother Marie, with an encouraging, Queen Elizabeth I, Catherine the Great-smile, a protective twinkle in her monarchical, feminine blue eyes. "Abbess will be ever-so delighted to see you obtain a University of Paris degree. Splendid, says Abbess, splendid! She herself never got beyond drawing and dancing lessons from her governess. By all means! Go for the goal with all your power! The University of Paris! Superb! Abbess looks forward to seeing Sweetheart included among such ladies as Marie Curie, Marina Tsvetaeva and Simone de Beauvoir!"

She clapped ladylike.

"Obtaining such a degree" concluded the Abbess, "will also bring much honor both to Cherie's own convent and to the entire Benedictine Order!"

Bless you! Bless you! Bless You! Bless you Mother Marie!" piped Sister Jeanne.

She immediately grasped and frantically kissed the abbess's right hand.

"I promise to do my very best, Mother Marie! I promise to study my very best!

"Abbess has no doubt you will."

"Bless you! Bless you, Mother Marie! I promise to make you proud!""

"Ah! Silly Abbess" observed the great lady. "Your Superior forgot to ask Cherie what Major she intends to take. Is it the same subject as on which Cherie based her outstanding Baccalaureate?"

"Oh yes, yes Mother Marie! I wish to receive a university degree in later Nineteenth Century French poetry. Verlaine, Rimbaud, Claudel, especially."

In demonstration, Sister Jeanne began reciting a poem by Verlaine: *"Les sanglot longs/Des violons–*

"Sh! Sh! Abbess believes you, Dear!" instructed the great lady, placing a reassuring, maternal right forefinger on the eager supplicant's mouth. "Sh! Abbess is confident her Sister Jeanne knows the entire poem by heart."

"Splendid, splendid!" the prioress continued. "What a knowledgeable little nun you are! Know that Abbess will pray daily for your outstanding success." She then repeating: "After all, your victory will not only be for yourself alone but for all your sisters both here in our convent and throughout the entire Benedictine Order."

"Bless you! Bless you! Bless you! Bless you Mother Marie!"

Still on her knees, Sister Jeanne once more frantically kissed the abbess's hand.

Affectionately, the great lady patted the novice on her teenage forehead.

Tears of joy raised Sister Jeanne's unmeddled-with cheeks.

"Bless you Mother Marie for being so kind as to remember my Baccalaureate g and for permitting me to take this university degree!

Yet on quaking adolescent knees, Sister Jeanne reached out to grip her Superior around the legs. She pressed against the abbess tight and close. She felt the abbess's shapely contours just beneath her habit. With the youngster's tearfully joyful face joined to her idol near waist, the two women just a decade apart in age, rocked gently back-and-forth. The pair, momentarily becoming as one body, one soul.

"Be careful darling, or you will damage your veil" interjected Sister Francoise.

The youngster instantly released the abbess.

She scrambled to her feet, swiftly readjusted her jumbled long skirts and her skewed wimple,

Soon, she fell on her knees again and frantically kissed Sister Francoise' hand.

"Sister Francoise! Sister Francoise! Don't ever doubt I love you too! I love you too! And love and seek your blessing just as much!

She desperate kissed this second great lady's right hand.

"There, there, darling. I've never once questioned your devotion to me."

"Please understand Sister Francoise" explained the youngster at last, her heart pounding. "It's simply that whenever I am permitted to speak to you two great ladies–that whenever you two great ladies exhibit interest in my fields of study–I become so-so worked up. I'm sorry but at those times I just can't control myself–I start to behave so crazy/"

"Fear not, darling" consoled Sister Francoise. "When Abbess and I were your age–not in fact so long ago–we too both got *worked up* over our interests. Interests, which were not far dissimilar from your own. We too at your age often started to *behave crazy*."

She patted the girl affectionately on tearful, unmeddled cheek.

"So true, so true!" interjected Mother Marie. "You and I once often acted just like this good little nun! Did we not, Francoise?"

"Yes, that was the primary reason I wanted the darling accepted into our convent" answered the abbess's soulmate. "Little Sister Jeanne reminds me so often of ourselves when we too were idealistic teenagers."

"Shall we?" Mother Marie asked her friend as each took the youngster by a separate hand.

"Yes"

"Alright. One–

"Two"

"Three–"

Wee!"

The Two Lovelies raised Sister Jeanne to feet.

Next, they further adjusted the girl's jumbled long skirts and skewed wimple.

"Go forth and study for your university degree, Cherie" instructed the abbess. "Remember too, we are all praying for your marvelous success, Cherie! Make us and our Order–as Abbess is fully confident you will–proud."

"Don't forget your Vows though, darling!" reminded Sister Francoise. "Make sure your studies do not interfere with your duties as a nun!"

"Bless you! Bless you!" bubbled Sister Jeanne, she making a deep curtsey and humble dip of head to each noble benefactress. "Bless you!

Bless you! I promise not to ever forget my duties as a nun. I promise to make you in all ways, proud of me!"

I

It was neither by chance or whim that *The Two Lovelies* chose bestowing their special favor upon little Sister Jeanne. While they originating from quite different social, class backgrounds, the great ladies and their supplicant had far more in common than might initially be imagined. Positions of power are lonely. Absolute power, even more so. There are few things people situated at these awesome but solitary heights desire more than a loyal, understanding friend. If the pair had exercised complete either indirect or official sovereignty over St. Elisabeth's Benedictine Convent for a decade, Mother Marie and Sister Francoise had no intimates but themselves. They, possessed no chum, no buddy save themselves in whom to open their hearts. The arrival of Sister Jeanne Navarro changed this. She offered *The Two Lovelies* their first opportunity to acquire this longed for individual. Not only was the youngster receptive to her Superior's yearning, she also resembled many aspects of the two ladies' own girlhood, Finally, Sweetheart appeared eager to fulfill many of her benefactress's most cherished hopes and dreams.

Marie-Therese-Adrienne-Michele de Valois-Martignac and Marie-Therese-Gabrielle-Francoise de Rousillon-Beaufort were near-inseparable companions since first meeting in Sunday School at age six. The two girls—they same: age; both strikingly pretty; each: a highly intelligent dainty cherry blond with soft, alluring voice; five-feet-five—were regularly mistaken for blood-sisters. Even for twins.

"I am yours, Francoise!" pledged one girl, when both aged twelve.

"And I am *yours*, Marie!" cried the other.

"From today and forever!"

"Yes, from today and forever!"

Each, straightened her companion's socks.

Next, the pair knelt solemnly on bare knees.

They kissed one another on lips
Embraced tight
Locks intertwining
Passionate nubile feminine bodies united.
Then, like Ruth and Naomi they made a sacred vow.
"Whatever you chose to become in life, or wherever you go in life, Francoise, I will become the same, I will go there, too!"
"Whatever you chose to become in life, or wherever you go in life, Marie, I will become the same, I will go there, too!"
"So help me God!"
"So help me too, God!"
"I am yours, Francoise!"
"And I am yours, Marie.
"We are as one girl from this day forth!
":Yes, Marie, we are now forever one girl."
"So help us together Blessed Virgin!"
"Amen."

If allowed, this gifted, idealistic feminine pair might go far in the world. As members of the enclosed, rarefied, self-perpetuating French aristocracy, this was not possible. "Daughters" insists the cultural doctrine this class obeys, "are not supposed to be educated. The less daughters know about the outside world and the less the outside world knows about them, the better!" Raised in such a restricted environment, girls during that era, no matter how: famous their name; elite their residence; or impressive their neglected-talent, raw mental abilities– confronted just three options in life: 1. A socially-acceptable marriage. 2. Enter a convent. 3. Become a pensioned-off *Maiden Aunt.* For uneducated younger daughters of *Old Rich* French Catholic families whose fortune was found more in–prestige; bankable name; trust fund; ownership of fine art; deeds to choice pieces of real estate; yacht; rather than immediate access to substantial cash–option 1. was restricted to their older sister.
What to do?
Which step to take?

Marie and Francoise–each girl clad in identical: navy blue monickered jacket; white blouse; short, light gray plaited skirt; white bobbysocks and black flats fastened at side with buckle; thick, long brown hair tied back with a big red satin bow–spent long hours together discussing their mutual future. They devoted much time to debating how the kids might resolve this thorny problem.

Finally, the chums reached a decision. As on all occasions arising since *The Two Lovelies* first met in Sunday School, they would confront the dilemma hand-in-hand.

"I am yours, Francoise!"

"And I am *yours*, Marie.

"We are as one girl from this day forth!

"Yes, Marie, we are now forever but as one girl."

"So help us together Blessed Virgin as if we were but one soul!"

"Amen"

Entering a convent did not sound particularly fun. By what the youngsters garnered from Mass, books, television and movies, becoming a nun involved living a secluded life where one: prayed; fasted; slept on a hard bed; felt guilty; chaperoned unruly brats; worked in a garden or at a soup kitchen."

"They also cut your hair short at the beginning!" winced Marie, adjusting her socks.

"Still, being a nun also brought long term benefits. It provided: personal honor; family admiration; respect from the community. A nun was guaranteed a home; social position; financial security.

"And your hair also goes grow back!" reminded Francoise, adjusting her socks.

"Think of Mother Berthe, for instance?" reminded Marie. "Remember how everyone dips his head or she curtseys to her? Remember, how Mother Berthe is so smart and knowledgeable and eager to hear all our stories! Everyone considers her wise and good? How everyone says: 'You ought to look to Mother Berthe as a noble example.' If we joined Mother Berthe's Order she would be ever-so delighted! She would go out of her way to train and guide us. Recount to us her wisdom! She'd make sure we wouldn't spend all our time taking care of brats or constantly feeling guilty about sins we didn't commit. Mother Berthe would make us good, socially-conscious nuns with a positive, constructive mission in life!"

"And that *always-hitting-you-with-a-ruler* stuff is only in stories" said Francoise.

In contrast, the kids considered the fate of their *Maiden Aunts* Eveline and Marcelle. Each one, condemned to Genteel Poverty–meager annual pension; torn, out-of-style dresses; once fashionable house now with pealing paint, leaky roof, cracked mirror, broken grandfather-clock; couch needing new springs; postbox jammed with unpaid bills. These two fomer belles-of-the-ball were today accompanied by gigolos to *Algerian War* veteran charity functions as they yammered-on about once being the one true love of Yves Montand or Gerard Depardieu.

"Ick!" exclaimed Marie. "No! I mean Double Ick! I love Auntie Eveline and I love Auntie Marcelle. Still, their lonely, disappointed lives remind me of Gloria Swanson in *Sunset Boulevard*!."

"The others in our families scoff about Auntie Eveline and Auntie Marcelle behind their back" recalled Francoise. "They tell nasty jokes about them."

"Auntie Eveline and Auntie Marcelle only get invited over on Christmas so that Papa and Mama won't feel guilty about ignoring them the rest of the year" added Marie.

"I've been told that when Auntie Eveline and Auntie Marcelle were our age'" said Francoise, "they were the very first girls hostesses invited to their balls, they were the very first girls hostesses asked to big occasions. I've been told that back then no ball, dinner or social event was ever considered "worthy" of mention on the society page or in the celebrity gossip column unless Auntie Eveline and Auntie Marcelle attended."

"Yet today" lamented Marie, "people who once did all they could to win their favor now claim they never once heard of Auntie Eveline or Auntie Marcelle!"

Which course in life ought a girl to take? Should she become a secluded but much honored, much loved nun, or should she become a lonely, eccentric *Blue Stocking*? The latter, forever dependent on her condescending, tight-fisted relatives. For Marie and Francoise, the answer was clear. Judging too, that as in the Armed Services, one goes farther through volunteering early rather than waiting to be drafted, the friends promptly announced the decision to their parents.

Delighted the kids were prepared going freely instead of being pressured, the two families took little time agreeing. In what later proved a lucky mix-up, the youngsters were dispatched not as intended to the close supervision of Carmelite Mother Berthe near Paris, but rather to the somewhat looser operated *St. Elisabeth's* Benedictine Convent far to the south in Hautes-Pyrénées Department.

Before embarking on this fateful journey, the two virgins embraced. Each, kneeling on her sixteen-year-old bare knees.

"I am yours, Francoise!"

"And I am *yours*, Marie.

"We are as one girl from this day forth!"

":Yes, Marie, we are now forever one girl."

"So help us together Blessed Virgin as if we were one soul.

"Amen"

These were the heady days of *Vatican II*. After being since at least 1789 a fortress of: defensive; inward-looking; political, academic and cultural reaction; a citadel instantly suspicious of any form of societal change–the Roman Catholic Church under Pope John XXIII at last tried to embrace not scorn modernity. Rome worked to adjust its ancient doctrines so they might be relevant and attractive to both believers and nonbelievers in a more liberal, ecumenical, religious, political and social age. Instead of fearing those who are different, the Church now eagerly sought others friendship. When Marie and Francoise entered St. Elisabeth's, they discovered an atmosphere in which the kids' personal qualities, especially their attribute of *Presence* could most easily bloom.

If dating back to early-Merovingian times, it been witness to many critical historical events, if possessed of priceless art, the convent our *Two Lovelies* entered was also a religious community in need of radical transformation and significant reform.

Like many of the people and places in France managing to survive the German Occupation during the Second World War, St. Elisbeth's and its older members harbored a recent unsavory past. Mother Agnes d'Hauteville, the woman serving as abbess from 1937 to 1959 only avoided prosecution as a collaborator following the Liberation though her intimate connections to powerful and similarly compromised members of the war's winning side. During the *Occupation,* Mother Agnes, while refusing to shelter Jewish women and children from German death squads or to hide downed Allied pilots or escaped POWS, often permitted Nazi officers to use her convent to hide plundered Jewish art works, bank accounts and other stolen property. In the closing months of the struggle, as German defeat approached, Mother Agnes also permitted St. Elisabeth's to serve as a way-station, a safe-house enabling some of history's most infamous war criminals to escape to Argentina.

If she taken a *Vow* of poverty, Mother Agnes was nonetheless well rewarded for her services. These payments coming indirectly through large gifts to her family's newspaper business and brother's real estate firm, through significant donations to the abbess's religious Order, by considerable bequests to her favored charities and free upkeep of her convent.

Although none of the other sisters were active collaborators, they were still clearly aware of their abbess's activities and made no effort to restrain or prevent them.

All the same, by 1960, when our story opens, St. Elisabeth's shady connection to the Germans was an unmentionable dirty secret shared by every man and woman alive in the Department during the Second World War. If none dared speak about it openly lest their own activities during the *Holocaust* be examined closely, people could still either retaliate or relieve a personal sense of guilt in other ways. By 1960, the once distinguished, prosperous, tourist-***Must See*** convent suffered substantial economic, material and workforce difficulties. If no local citizen or regional office-seeker dared speak out against the cloistered-collaborators, they could at least deny the nuns further financial aid, cease visiting this once hallowed-institution, discourage all press, tourist, or academic attention, refrain from continuing to offer up to the convent their younger daughters. By 1960, St. Elisabeth's found itself steeped in debt, ignored by reporters, tourists and scholars, its structure in need of major repair, the average age of its steadily-diminishing community of sisters risen to over fifty-five.

Ironically, when sixteen-year-old Marie de Valois-Martignac and Francoise de Rousillon-Beaufort arrived at St. Elisbeth's that autumn, they found themselves in a position to remedy the unhappy situation. And do so, with a speed and to an extent thought only possible in each one's wildest, teenage dreams. If the pair now had no choice but to spend the rest of their lives behind convent walls, this secluded existence actually offered them far more freedom of action, provided the girls immensely wider room to express their personal artistic and intellectual gifts than would ever be permitted in the elitist, "Daughters should not be educated" environment from which this dynamic duo came.

"They cut your hair short at the beginning!" winced Marie at her *Robing* as she was dressed as a novice, observing the mounds of her dark brown locks collected on the cold, white marble floor.

"Yet it grows back even thicker" answered Francoise as the wimple was placed atop her equally shorn head at the same ceremony.

"And when it does grow back" replied Marie, sensing the hair she lost was also the severed cord once binding the girl to her original constricted society, "we will be free to make our own decisions."

II

"Let the two young ladies try" suggested Abbess Marguerite Sandoval, the often fainthearted successor to Mother Agnes. "These kids are so eager to undertake the attempt."

With those words, Marie and Francoise went to work with their plans to personally revitalize the community both physically and spiritually. The Benedictine Order establishing each convent or monastery as an independent, no fuddy-duddy male clerical *higher-ups* were able to interfere with the girls' strategy.

Marie began by leading the other nuns in daily exercises, as well as daily practices of yoga and jogs around the convent's substantial grounds. These endeavors were soon followed by contests to discover which of the sisters could swiftest reshine the pews in the public chapel, which lady could easiest spruce-up the objects on the altars, she most ably dust-off the statuary and stained glass.

Francoise provided extra encouragement by unfurling her guitar and singing Woodie Guthrie, Jimmie Rodgers and Carter Family songs. Too bad she never made it to the *Grand Ole Oprey* in Nashville. She would have become a star. The young nun possessed an ever so sweet, forever memorable feminine voice. One, which projected her fine, beckoning renditions of these ballads throughout the Medieval edifice.

By the following January, 1961, it was clear that the torch had been passed to new generation; that the Sisters of St. Benedict should "ask not what my convent can do for me" but rather, "what I can do for my convent?"

With no clerical *Bay of Pigs* or religious Vietnam on the horizon, one might with confidence predict St. Elisabeth's was soon to become another *Camelot*, even a true *Great Society*.

It wasn't long until Marie and Francoise found they too each possessed an unexploited knack for business. While the *Rule* of St. Benedict dating to the Sixth Century instructed each of his monastic communities (both male and female) to be self-supporting, St. Elisabeth's permitted this clause to lapse after 1945. During the succeeding fifteen years, the local merchants given the contracts to supply the cloistered nuns with food, hardware supplies and other goods regularly cheated them on prices. Taking command of the convent's business accounts, the two novices sought to remedy the sorry situation.

These two habited, veiled bookkeepers, Crucifix and *Rosary* around each girl's slender neck and short waist, swiftly eliminated all the *Sweetheart-Deals, No-Show Jobs.* double-payments, deliveries of spoiled or passed-selling-date items, and cross-responsibility tasks. All this long established yet easily avoidable red tape bit deeply into the convent's meager bank account. Henceforth: all fruit and vegetables, all poultry, baked and dairy products, were to be grown and produced within the convent. Hardware, electrical repair, plumbing. and dry cleaning were also to come strictly from this same venue. Besides saving a tremendous amount of money, these economic reforms did much to give the other nuns a renewed sense of responsibility as well as awaken each woman's long dormant personal talents. Miranda Navarro eagerly chipped-in by providing a regular supply of fish from the river on her farm back at San Pedro/St. Pierre. As Francoise with her guitar started playing Bob Dylan ballads, it soon became clear both within the convent and in the adjoining towns, that something new and inspiring was indeed: *Blowing in the Wind,* that following over a decade-and-a half of moral, spiritual, physical decline, St. Elisabeth's could now proudly say: *The times, they are achanging.*

Next, Marie and Francoise investigated the overseen financial potential available to their community in other sectors. The convent's huge library and vast archives intricately recording the history of Benedictine nuns in France since the early Middle Ages fell into dusty neglect during the *Occupation.* Following a thorough cleaning, good spruce-up and fine re-cataloging, this gold mine of information was again made available (with either a recommended one-time visitor's donation or a suggested annual contribution) to all grad students, researchers, writers and journalists. This done, the convent's remarkable architecture and sculpture collections were opened to paid-guided public tours, to photographers, filmmakers and to art enthusiasts.

Finally, St. Elisabeth's *Moor, Romanesque, Gothic* and *Baroque* outer quadrangle and defensive parapets were rented to form the backdrop in first French and later international drama, television and movie productions. Thrilled to feel they were now part of such a grand historic and art tradition, the big-name celebrities appearing in these films eagerly provided the convent significant monetary grants. Part of this Hollywood funding was used to open a free day care center and medical clinic. Both innovations provided valuable assistance to the local mountain villages. These long under-served inhabitants previously needed to travel a considerable distance to reach similar preschool and doctor facilities in Toulouse and other major lowland towns.

Thanks to the girls' reforms, St. Elisabeth's achieved that condition so immensely rare among religious establishments—no debt. Word quickly spread and a community once shunned, avoided, became again a tourists-**Must See** and a cherished haven for scholars. It wasn't long too before the many noted theologians and other famous academics benefiting from the vast but hitherto underused resources in the archives started publishing major work based on their research. A small but increasingly influential periodical concerning religion in the Twentieth Century was also founded at the convent. Marie and Francoise decided to call the distinguished magazine they established *Faith Today*.

Yet far more than economic revitalization, intellectual notoriety popular appeal were achieved under *The Two Lovelies*. While most Roman Catholic female religious institutions during the *Vatican II* period experienced a haemorrhage of membership, St. Elisabeth's soon found herself confronted with far more requests for entrance than she knew what to do with! If the average age of the sisters was fifty-five when Marie and Francoise arrived, under the two's' energetic, younger generation guidance that median dropped to less than thirty! Now, rather than uneducated, cast-off extra daughters, many of the novices were professionals, university graduates, even holders of advanced degrees. *In that jingle-jangle morning*, the newcomers assured the pair, *I'll keep following you.*

If many a recent arrival came to St. Elisabeth's seeking–either: a haven to recover from deep personal troubles; because she viewed the convent as a place in which to better focus her intellectual, artistic gifts; or, because she considered the quiet, secluded institution a shelter where she could more adequately learn her duty to a greater world–rather than to fulfill a religious *Vocation* in the strict, traditional sense–Marie and Francoise were not concerned. "What is a *Calling* after all," the community's two young leaders asked. "A summons to serve God comes to each of us in different, often mysterious guises, shapes and forms. So long as each new individual was sincere in her desire to serve the Almighty, that was is all which mattered.

Soon, Mother Marguerite gave up her position and was succeeded by Marie de Valois-Martignac. This relatively recent arrival to the community became the youngest person to hold that distinguished office the Benedictine's long history. If she could, Marie would have made Francoise de Roussillon-Beaufort co-leader. This not possible under the *Rule*, she appointed her closest friend since Sunday School: Sub-Abbess.

"*Mother Marie*" giggled the youthful prioress, she deeply honored but also a bit embarrassed at so swiftly winning her new office. "*Mother Marie*. That sounds so goofy. I'm not old enough to be anyone's–*mother*."

III

A truly historic era now unfolded.

One, providing a warm, beckoning light amidst the darkness so often the *Sixties*.

It was a period offering the entire world spiritual and intellectual enlightenment.

This was quite an achievement for the two girls considered. Especially, considering that neither kid had a single day of formal education. Both, renown theological figures today, each, originally entered the cloister simply because her relatives gave their younger daughters no alternative.

The stone which the builders rejected became the cornerstone.

Yet as this celebrated time progressed, its pretty architects grew ever more uneasy, mentally restless.

What next should this unique pair devote their one united-heart, dedicate the two's single, undivided soul?

"As each year passes" confessed Mother Marie to Sister Francoise, "I sense more becoming like one of those scientists, scholars, or artists who grasp their finest prize before reaching middle age. Then, spend the rest of her life just making speeches, writing articles, getting honorary degrees that celebrate victories won long ago."

"Yes, I know exactly what you mean, Cherie."

If they were both less than thirty, the two girls following their strenuous mental labors, each felt inwardly much older.

"We've together set this fruitful new era firmly in artful, intellectual motion, Francoise. It can now go on without our direct help. People around the world continue to claim all the success at St. Elisabeth's is entirely due to us alone. Well, maybe that was true at the beginning, but today you and I are just resting on our collective laurels."

"What can we do now to be more that just honored spectators, Marie"

"I'm not sure, Francoise."

"Let's pray on it."

"Yes, let's pray on it.

"We two pray as if we are one girl."

"Yes, we two pray as if we are one girl."

"Amen"

Then, as if in answer to the pair's request, novice Jeanne came upon the scene.

"I can't believe I was originally dubious about accepting the girl!" admitted Mother Marie to Sister Francoise. "Silly me! It certainly was not long before all my misgivings about her evaporated. The girl is precisely who we need to be our eventual successor–to be the girl who will continue our spiritual tradition here at St. Elisabeth's. The girl reminds me of just how we were ourselves at her age."

The girl?

If *The Two Lovelies* were in fact only nine years older than Juana Navarro/Sister Jeanne, a decade of directing and shaping the renewal of St. Elisabeth's Convent made Mother Marie and Sister Francoise sense they were not just the new arrival's older siblings but rather her parents.

A bright canary yellow orb ascended into cloudless aquamarine sky

Apple and cherry trees were in full soft pink blossom

Tulips, crocus, hyacinths, magnolias, anemones forming a riot of primary colors.

Songbirds delivered their aria.

From the east, blew a gentle, restful breeze

.Soon after granting the novice permission to obtain a degree from the University of Paris, Mother Marie retired to her cell to write a letter. It was one, the abbess sent biweekly to her young cousin, the heiress to their historic clan's title and fortune. At seventeen, the youngster was also Sister Jeanne's own age. Not yet become the celebrated, multi-Olympic Gold Medal winning "Fleet-footed Duchess," adolescent Raymonde de

Valois-Martignac was then being raised at the Benedictine convent in Normandy. Where, she was often found scurrying about the ancient institution's *Gothic* quadrangle. Nearby, her first coach, Sister Madeleine Beauchamp–*Rosary* in one hand, stopwatch in the other–urged the young aspirant on. "Faster Dear, faster! Put all your body and soul into it, Cherie! Remember, Carpe Diem! Seize the Day! Don't forget: 'To the winner go the spoils'! 'Victory comes to those who dare!' Seize history by the throat and make her your own!"

Raymonde, or to intimates: *Rose, Rosalie*, lost both parents when only a child and her first cousin, Marie, although nine years older and a cloistered nun who never actually met the orphan, felt a deep obligation to serve as the girl's special counselor and protector. She, choosing to perform that duty even if her unique advise and loving guardianship might only be provided from a distance. This surrogate *mother-daughter* relationship did much to fill an emptiness in the abbess's heart. Marie knew that if she was a bride of Christ, her husband, no matter how affectionate and tender He might be to His loyal mate, was still forever physically distant in this present mortal world.

Continued reliance on a computer tends causing the quality of one's handwriting to deteriorate. Once excellent manicured lines decay into indecipherable jumble. Mother Marie, however, retained the same graceful feminine calligraphy she acquired in childhood. Not only considered a major contemporary religious figure, the abbess is praised too for her skill with ink or pencil. The nun's distinctive, ever-cogent script possesses the same matchless twists, turns, jumps and loops as Golbihar Kermanshani performing on the Olympic figure skating rink.

St. Elisabeth's, April 13

Dearest Rose, thank you so very much for remembering my birthday. I promise to keep the lovely card you made for me, on my desk. There, it may be treasured until my dying day. I know the other sisters too will be impressed with your art skill. I was originally going to call you as usual "Little Rose" until realizing my cousin is now a big girl. Pardon me, a real, proper, young LADY! One, who will soon grow rightly tired of receiving all my incessant, unrequested maternal advise. Still, please try bearing with me, Cherie. As the closest thing I will ever possess to a child of my own, you must understand it is impossible for me to resist deluging Darling with motherly care and worry. Just in case Sister Madeleine is becoming jealous of my interference, please tell her that I enclose with this message a brand new stopwatch and a leather cover notebook so she can better record your remarkable running ability.

The pretty writer stopped.

Set down her fountain-pen

Adjusted her skirt.

She mused for a minute or two.

Beyond the window to left, songbirds extolled

A canary yellow orb in aquamarine sky, smiled

The writer now again took up her fountain-pen.

Uniform scratch of sentences recorded on paper resounded firm but gentle.

Oh yes, your silly big cousin forgot to mention it earlier! I enclose in this message too a photograph of one of my convent's newest member. She is named Sister Jeanne and is also your age. I hope one day that you two talented girls can meet. I know you pair will become instant soulmates as did Francoise and I. As my own Cherie is destined to become a great athlete and a noble LADY, Sister Jeanne is destined to develop into a famous daughter of Christ. I pray you Dears can soon cross paths. If God wills that encounter to occur, please be good and helpful to Sister Jeanne. I promise by all that's holy you will never regret it. I promise you will always treasure your new special friend.

Always loving you, Mother Marie de Valois-Martignac OSB

UNDER THE
PALM OF DEBORAH

"*L*ook Mama! Look! See what just came for me in the mail!" exclaimed Sister Jeanne, displaying the diploma she just received from the University of Paris. This prestigious document, printed with elaborate, antique script on parchment arrived in the morning post. Each day save in rain or heavy snow, daughter and mother communed beneath a shading, embracing evergreen tree in the convent garden. Child was seated atop a blue wooden bench, Parent, rested in her grave beneath a shined granite marker.

> *Maria-Miranda Navarro'*
> *XXXX to XXXX*
> *"I did my damnedest"–Harry Truman*

The delft-blue sky was cloudless, the fluorescent sun bright, the air fresh. These factors, along with wide evergreens and springtime's blooming crocus, roses, tulips, lilies, phlox, camellias, peturias, forsythias, hollyhocks, delphiniums, anemones, hyacinths, pansies, scillas made this ancient, convent garden a riot of vivid, living, primary colors.

"My degree is in later-Nineteenth and early Twentieth Century French poetry, Mama. I especially concerned myself with the work of Verlaine, Rimbaud, Paul Claudel and Valery–And see, Mama! I also graduated the very top in my class! If you wish, I'll read you my treatise. All my professors were most impressed with it."

As she author prepared to read her distinguished composition aloud, she reflected, "I guess those smacks Mama so frequently delivered to my fanny came to good use."

"Splendid! Splendid!" injected Sister Francoise, approaching from behind, she followed by several other members of the community. "Just as I expected! When Abbess and I granted you permission to apply for the degree, we both already knew you would do magnificently! The very first in your class! Just as you earlier came out among the top 1% taking the Baccalaureate examination! It's yet another brilliant success not only for you Cherie personally, but for the entire benedictine Order."

The newcomers all clapped in vigorous demonstration of ladylike support.

Sister Jeanne became embarrassed.

She cringed.

Looked away, demure.

Blushed crimson.

Next, she began delivering a gesture of both thanks and humility.

Sister Francoise, speedily insisted the young scholar cheer-up and remain seated.

"No, no, Cherie. Stay seated! Don't feel embarrassed. It is *my* obligation. It is your sisters *obligation* to honor you!"

Sister Francoise and the other nuns bowed to their gifted young colleague.

Once more, all the nuns eagerly clapped in genteel team approval

Soon too, they all giggled and jumped-up-and-down in place to further demonstrate admiration.

All, jumping-up-and-down as much as wearing habits and their assumption of a religious *Vocation* both permitted and deemed proper.

"What do you plan doing next, Cherie?"

"If I'm permitted, I'd like to continue my studies and acquire a graduate degree."

"Of course you may Cherie" replied Sister Francoise, fond twinkle in brown eyes.

She paused..

"On just one condition, however."

"What's that, Sister Francoise?"

"That you permit Abbess and I to publish your papers in our monthly journal."

"Seriously, Sister Francoise?"

"Oh yes indeed, Cherie! Abbess and I are most impressed with your highly readable, most informative and charming scholarship. We think it is precisely what our journal needs to win a large audience."

Sister Francoise paused, a wide smile arising on her strikingly pretty face.

"Abbess and I will of course give full credit to Cherie's work."

"What can I say" responded Sister Jeanne, humble.

"Then may I presume you accept the condition for your further study?"

"Yes, you may Sister Francoise."

"As I thought."

The superior pecked the bookish little novice affectionately on her soft, un-meddled with right cheek.

"Cherie's acceptance comes too with a promotion. She will henceforth be raised from novice to one of our community's full, voting member. Congratulations!"

Sister Jeanne instinctively curtseyed deep.

"I hope I will do you and the others rightly proud."

I

One

Two

Three

Four

Five

Six

Seven

Eight–major articles on early modern French poetry authored by little Sister Jeanne Navarro OSB appeared in the pages of succeeding issues of St. Elisabeth's journal *Faith Today*. "These essays" wrote *L'Express*, "are truly ground-breaking in both insightful original scholarship and in first rate literary composition." "Each piece" extolled *Liberation*, "brilliantly reveals and analyzes a new and heretofore overlooked aspect of a subject widely considered long since resolved." "Above all" said *Le Matin*, "these articles are written in a uniquely-compelling, illuminating and entertaining style." "It is a form of presentation" insisted Great Britain's *Spectator*, "sure to win their author the lasting admiration of both distinguished professors and casual readers." "Each essay boasts all the primary research and numerous footnotes required to placate ever-critical **experts**" accurately predicted the UK's *Evening Standard*. "All, are composed in a similar engaging, piquant manner. These celebrated treatises (later appearing in bestseller book form with all profits going to the Benedictine Order) should swift capture the avid, lasting imagination of both academia and the general reading public." The fact this book was the work of a shy, young, unknown, cloistered nun served to yet further intrigue a continually expanding readership.

"See! I told you the youngster would bring your convent tremendous honor!" Bishop Gautier could not resist boasting to Mother Marie, she once dubious about accepting the teenager into her religious community..

"Maybe we girls both missed our true calling?" giggled Sister Francoise to her soulmate. "Maybe we should really have been press barons–I mean *baronesses*!"

"Joseph Pulitzer and Lord Beaverbrook in habits!" tittered Mother Marie, plaintive.

Begun as a mere weekly newsletter designed to bolster the sagging spirits of one regional institution thought long passed its prime, *Faith Today* soon became, thanks largely to Sister Jeanne's immense yet previous unexploited writing talent, a periodical read wide and devotedly across the entire nation. The journal was subscribed to by free-thinkers no less than by determined believers. The magazine continued to be praised not just for the liberal, open-minded stance it always took when presenting Roman Catholicism, but also for the superb quality of its investigative reporting. *Faith Today* became remarkable not just as a standard bearer of ecumenical religious thought but also as a source for the latest, most insightful literary and historic research.

"I hope you are happy with the path in life to which I was called, Mama?" queried Sister Jeanne as she and Miranda once more communed in the garden, beneath the stately evergreen tree.

II

Tap, tap, tap, even, steady tap-of dedicated, mid-twenties, feminine, flat shoes.

Scurry, scurry, scurry—of teenage sneakers eager to keep up with beloved leader.

Sound of the pair's tread resonating on Medieval granite floor

"Of course one shouldn't get cubbyholed into a single era or subject, Cherie" advised Abbess as she escorted *Faith Today*'s star correspondent along the off-white and sand-brown Moorish arcade situated near the convent's main quadrangle.

"I agree with you completely, Mother Marie!" answered Sister Jeanne, she hurrying to keep up.

"Abbess is always speaking in Cherie's best interests."

"Of course, Mother Marie."

"After all, you are such a gifted child."

"I hope I can live up to your expectations, Mother Marie."

"Abbess knows her Jeannette will far exceed them!"

"Bless you, Mother Marie!"

Tap, tap, tap, even steady, dedicated tap of adult feminine shoes

Scurry, scurry, scurry, eager to keep-up teenage sneakers scurrying

Pair's walk resonating far on Medieval granite.

If her maternal love for young cousin Raymonde or Rose, Duchess de Charpentier was undiminished, the daily physical presence of little Sister Jeanne permitted Abbess to more forthright express a similar yearning.

Upon reaching the end of the long, stone covered, stone walkway, the prioress opened a heavy oak door and motioned for she and protegée to enter.

"Follow me, Dear. Abbess has something to show you—something Abbess is confident you will find most intriguing!"

Behind the barrier was a spacious, vault--ceiling, if slightly musty enclosure. One, the size of either an Olympic swimming pool arena or a professional basketball venue. Located in the middle, was a long row of: straight-backed, wicker-bottomed chairs set under oak writing desks with long, slender-necked metal lamps. It was all similar to the furniture Sister Jeanne remembered when as bobysocker Mademoiselle Juana Navarro, she was in research libraries preparing for the Baccalaureate examination. Along its walls, from stucco, brown, tiled floor to white paint ceiling sixteen meters above, the in-between area divided into three levels, each with wrought-iron floor, steps and bannister, were to be seen the archives of France's Benedictine nuns.

"Awesome!" exclaimed Sister Jeanne as she looked about.

Even though a significant number of documents were lost or destroyed in 1789, the surviving files, some dating back into the mists of Merovingian times, still covered every inch of available shelf space. Exactly how many precious historic letters, diaries, books, files, charts and other documents, some so old and frail they might crumble at human touch, were preserved in this room? Only God knew for sure.

"Awesome!" piped Sister Jeanne, eagerly darting her excited adolescent eyes in all directions. "Awesome! No, *really* awesome!"

"That's exactly the reaction I knew Cherie would have!" responded Mother Marie. Her strikingly pretty face projected a warm, beckoning glow.

Abbess looked on proudly, sporting a wide grin of maternal satisfaction as *Faith Today*'s star correspondent raced about the library. The girl, glancing this-way-and-that, she speeding right-and-left, up-and-down-and-around, lunging along every possible book shelf. She, desperate to investigate every inch of the learned material her joyous, inquisitive, adolescent eyes could find.

"Awesome! No, *really* awesome!"

Not until Sister Jeanne was thoroughly exhausted, completely out of breath, her heart and lungs recklessly speeding, did she at last come to a much regretted worn-out halt. The girl dropping into one of the straight-backed, wicker chairs to spend several minutes recovering her composure.

"That's exactly the reaction I knew Cherie would have!" repeated Mother Marie, gleefully. She, delivering her talented liege a fond peck on right unmeddled-with cheek.

"After several weeks of strenuous effort, I managed getting the documents into some *Scatterbrained Female* degree of cataloging" injected Mother Marie apologetically, her elegant speech shifting unconsciously into *First Person*. "So when you begin investigating the material it won't be a total leap into the **Great Unknown**."

A couple of the stucco floor tiles were loose.

Areas of the ceiling needed repainting.

The light-bulb of one of the table-lamps needed replacing.

"Still, as you see, I couldn't get everything fixed before I brought you here" admitted Mother Marie, with apologetic smile, motion of her arms and upper body beseeching surrogate-daughter's forgiveness.

"Oh, considering all that you were up against, Mother Marie" swift assured the teenage bookworm, she still bent in a wicker chair recovering her breath, "you did an awesome job of renovation and cataloging."

"Thank you, Cherie. It might run in the blood. My grandmother was the chief librarian at the Biblioteque Nationale in Paris."

"I'm not surprised, Mother Marie. You are following in a family tradition."

"That's kind of you, Child."

Sister Jeanne at last won back her physical composure. She rose to her feet and the two virgins embarked on a leisurely stroll about the library. The pair, were oblivious to to the periodic bump of a loose floorboard or the random creak of an un-oiled door hinge.

The archives contained an intricate record of the life of Benedictine nuns in France going back to when they first arrived in what was then called Frankish Gaul. No other institution, secular or religious, public or private, boasted such a large, wide, deep and elaborate compilation.

"It was" thought Sister Jeanne, surveying this latter day-Library of Alexandria, "as if all the members of my Order going back to Merovingian days magically understood a contemporary sister was going to write our clan's story and therefore collected all the information needed so that future author might tell our tale in its multi-sided cultural and historic glory."

"Some reporters from the *Associated Press, AFP* and *Reuters* already asked me if they might look at these papers," said Mother Marie, she still addressing her surrogate-daughter in *First Person*. "However, I told them I wanted giving my gifted protegée a chance to study them, first."

She giggled.

Pressed Sister Jeanne's right hand tight, affectionately.

"Controlling entry and access is one of the benefits coming with being an abbess. I've got as-it-were: *'the keys-to-the-kingdom.'*"

"So it is—so you do, Mother Marie."

"Anyway" pursued the lovely maiden gatekeeper, "it is most important for my Cherie not to allow herself to be cubby-holed, to be boxed-into just a single niche of literary or historical investigation. You don't wish to become similar to one of those *Hollywood* actors, actresses like Jack Nicholson or Meg Ryan who basically play the same general role in movie after movie!"

"No indeed, Mother Marie. You wish me to expand, to take on many, varied parts—like Daniel Day-Lewis or Emma Thompson, as it were."

"Good, good! That's a good girl. You get the drift of my meaning."

Mother Marie absent-minded twirled her *Rosary*.

Your essays on early modern French poetry are brilliant, splendid!" she said. "They are delicious to take up again and again! So informative and so fun to read! To read over and over! No law exists declaring that scholarly research must always be as dry as Pharaoh's tomb!"

"As the sales of our *Faith Today*" continued the fetching door guard, "as the public's increasing appetite for your little book, as the avid praise of those highbrow-receding-hairline, paid-to-find-fault big-name critics all demonstrate, you have clearly captured writing fame, distinction and success. It's a fame, distinction and success Cherie is not going to forfeit any time soon. Certainly not if her Mama—I mean *Abbess*—possesses the slightest say in the matter!"

"Mi!" the abbess purred with satisfaction, absent-mindedly twirling her *Rosary*. "How much help my Jeannette already has brought to our Order! Soon, a small portion of the profits Baby's little volume brought-in from just its first month of sale will be enough to transform all the dusty files and documents Cherie observes his morning into safely secured videotape!. I may even install a commemorative plaque."

Mother Marie pressed her surrogate-daughter's right hand affectionately tight.

"However to my mind" she said, "Cherie's authorship career should now be just beginning. Her magnificent set of essays on French poetry ought to be only the preliminary salvo in her great literary cannonade."

"I'm glad you have such trust in my talents, Mother Marie," ventured her companion.

"Oh, indeed I do, Sweetheart. I wouldn't have brought you here today unless I was already sure of your ability to: 'take the high ground,' to: 'capture the citadel.' " Then after pause, the lady confided: My mother's side of my family were often generals. That's where I picked up all these military euphemisms."

The abbess once more twirled her *Rosary*.

Suspecting the direction in which her Superior's train of thought was heading, the youngster again contemplated the book shelves.

Ooh! Awesome! *Really* awesome! What a chance!"

"It was" thought Sister Jeanne under her breath, she further surveying this latter day-Library of Alexandria, "as if all the members of my Order going back to Merovingian days magically understood a contemporary sister was going to write our clan's story. They therefore collected all the information needed for that later author to tell our tale in its every cultural and historic glory.".

"And the sisters of yore collected it all so that our Order's cultural and historic glory" reflected the teenager, hopeful, "might be authored by little *me*."

"To demonstrate to both the general reading public and to the receding-hairline professors that my Cherie is a girl of many notable interests, of many unique gifts, I hereby instruct her to compose an analysis of these archives."

"That's a tremendous honor, Mother Marie!" tweedled Sister Jeanne, with delight.

"Just as I thought my Darling would react!"

"*Rome wasn't built in a day.* It will certainly take a while if you wish me to produce essays about our sisters written with the same literary quality as I produced ones on Verlaine, Rimbaud, Claudel and Valery!"

"Naturally, of course, Sweetheart. One doesn't pop-out essays of your quality in an instant. *Rome wasn't built in a day*"

"Bless you Mother Marie! Bless you, Mother Marie!" cried her young protegée. "I was so hoping this was the reason why you brought me this awesome library! Bless you! Bless you! Bless you, Mother Marie! I promise, promise, promise I won't let you down!"

"I know Darling won't let me down! Try not to exhaust yourself on the way, though, Honey. Remember: as Benjamin Franklin said: *All work and no play makes Jack*–or rather Jeanne–*a dull girl.*"

"Yes, but also don't forget–*Idle hands are the devil's playthings.*"

The youngster hugged the lady tight, showered her with heartfelt kisses.

In the process, she almost knocking off both her own and the heroine's wimples.

Sister Jeanne was anything but–Silent *as a nun.*

"A major reason why I put-off the *Associated Press* and other reporters" explained Mother Marie, readjusting her habit and wimple, "is because I believe our archives first need to be investigated by a fellow woman. Sure, men can get all the facts recorded correctly. However, it takes another woman to truly understand what it meant to be–what it *means* to be a member of our Order. I therefore chose you to assume the sacred, as Cherie would say–*awesome*–task."

"Bless you! Bless You! Bless you, Mother Marie! I promise, promise, promise I won't let you down!'"

Once more, the girl hugged the lady tight, showered her with heartfelt kisses.

In the process, she almost knocking off both her own and heroine's wimples.

"As the Abbess of St. Elisabeth's" instructed Mother Marie, readjusting both her own and her sidekick's outfits, "I henceforth absolve you of performing all but your most sacred responsibilities as a member of this community until you complete your next set of writings. There are after all many ways to serve as God's instrument. The Almighty has clearly selected Cherie to spread His message in a less conventional manner."

"Bless you, Bless you—"

"Yes, yes Sweetheart. Mama gets the point. Now take up your pen!"

III

One
Two
Three
Four
Five
Six
Seven
Eight
Nine
Ten
Eleven
Twelve—major articles recording the multifaceted history of Benedictine nuns in France since the early Middle Ages appeared in the pages of *Faith Today*. Once more, all were written by Sister Jeanne Navarro OSB, the same teenager responsible for the previous much critically acclaimed and immensely popular series on early modern French poetry.

"Without doubt" declared *Figaro*, "this young writer is no mere one-trick creative writing pony. She's no simple flash in the book sale pan. Yet again, her work is ground-breaking in both insightful original scholarship and in first rate literary conception." .

"A subject–French Medieval Benedictine nuns–likely to at first strike both general readers and even academics as rather pedantic, wonky" said *Le Monde*, "is transformed by a masterful storyteller into an account as fascinating, as exciting, as difficult to set down as the best classical novel or fast-paced thriller"

"To the extent this monastic Order has been studied at all in recent decades, attention has been directed almost entirely to its male section" wrote Great Britain's *Guardian*. "However since the publication of Sister Jeanne Navarro's excellent both learned and highly entertaining articles, this regrettable oversight is no more."

"The stories are each a masterpiece!" cooed the normally sedate *London Times*. "Thanks to Sister Jeanne's latest brilliant and absorbing account, her fellow nuns are shown to have included across the centuries many noted and influential writers, scientists, inventors, doctors, painters, diplomats, even singers. At last, thanks to the author's masterful pen, these ladies are given their rightful due, are celebrated as they have so long deserved."

"Sister Jeanne's newest articles" glowed Germany's *Deutsche Zeitung*, "are once more a product of her signature compelling, her uniquely entertaining but also wise, ever thought-provoking brand of literature."

"It is a new artful creative writing technique" according to the *New Yorker*, "sure to win the author and her literary children the lasting admiration of both distinguished professors and casual readers."

"Each one based on primary research and armed with the footnotes required to placate critical **experts**, all, fashioned in a similar engaging, zesty manner, these celebrated treatises" predicted Spain's *El Pais* correctly, "will swift capture the avid, lasting imagination of both academia and the general reading public."

"Ooh! Wow! Super! Awesome! No, no, I mean really awesome!" piped the author upon she reading the reviews.

As with her earlier series on French poetry, Sister Jeanne's newer articles too soon appeared compiled in bestseller book form with all profits going to the Benedictine Order. "They form a volume" proclaimed the *New York Times*, "which anyone possessing a serious interest in history should not dare miss."

"The fact this superb book is written by a shy, young, cloistered nun" wrote Italian *Corriere Della Sara*, "serves to yet further intrigue her continually expanding readership. She is in the process of becoming an intellectual St. Therese of Lisieux, maybe even a Roman Catholic Anne Frank."

"See! See! See! I promised I wouldn't let you down, Mother Marie!" pledged Sister Jeanne, holding her patroness tight, showering her idol with heartfelt kisses.

"Yes, yes, Mama knew Baby wouldn't ever let me—let the world down—Cherie," responded the Abbess, tears of maternal love running her strikingly pretty face.

As before, *Faith Today* itself benefited immensely from Sister Jeanne's talent. The journal became subscribed to not simply throughout the European continent but was soon as well captured devoted readers on both sides of the Atlantic Ocean. It is read avidly by free-thinkers no less than by determined believers. The magazine continues to be praised not just for the liberal, open-minded stance it always took when presenting Roman Catholicism, but also for the superb quality of its investigative reporting. *Faith Today* is remarkable" expounded *The Washington Post*, "not just as a standard bearer of ecumenical religious thought but also as a source for the latest, most insightful literary and historic research." Still, when *The Two Lovelies* announced that St. Elisabeth's would soon hold a series of televised public seminars concerning the role of women and religion in the present age, *The New York Review of Books* spoke for many around the world in saying: "Now, At last we will be provided a chance to meet Sister Jeanne."

IV

"Well, we've tried to keep little Jeanette all to ourselves" conceded Sister Francoise, "but I guess that couldn't last forever."

"Yes, we tried to keep little Jeannette all to ourselves" reiterated Mother Marie, "but I guess that couldn't last forever."

"Anyway" reminded Sister Francoise, "avarice is a Deadly Sin."

"So true" sighed Mother Marie."Avarice is a Deadly Sin."

It is our duty to let all her devoted readers discover what their favorite author actually looks like is.

"As Christ says," reminded Abbess: *"It is more blessed to give than to receive."*

"Amen."

Following the international sensation created by the cloistered author's brilliant literary work, it was inevitable sufficient pressure would be placed on *St. Elisabeth's* to finally present their celebrated young member to the public.

"This way, Sweetheart" instructed Mother Marie, as she took her gifted sidekick firmly by right arm. "Come with us."

"Yes, this way, Darling" explained Sister Francoise, taking her talented protegée steadfast by left arm. "Come with us."

The young author was escorted by her two patronesses into St. Elisabeth's public church with its: stunning 40-meter *Gothic* vault decorated with Poussin murals; *Cordoba* arabesque flooring; *Baroque* marble, gold and silver altar sculpted by Bernini and painting of the ascending Virgin crafted by Rubens. This too, was the place where Mademoiselle Navarro was first taken into the Benedictine Order. Today, also marked the first time Sister Jeanne ventured outside the cloister in over two years. Save for her conversations with Miranda behind the grille, her daughter never encountered any member of the lay community since she taking the veil. For someone grown accustomed to living in seclusion, this new experience was to say the least, unnerving.

Snap, snap, snap, snap, snap, snap—additional newspaper photographer snaps.

Whir, hum. steady buzz of CNN, BBC, PBS television cameras.

Correspondents from AP, AFP, Reuters, El Mundo all straining to be recognized.

"Yes, yes Messieurs and Mesdames" announced Sister Aimée, she serving as St. Elisabeth's press secretary. "The Child has agreed to be interviewed. But please understand this is Cherie's first experience with such a situation. Please try to be thoughtful and ask your questions in a calm, respectable manner. I promise .all those raising their queries as gentlemen and ladies will receive the relies they seek."

Snap, snap, snap, snap, snap, snap—additional newspaper photographer snaps.

Whir, hum, steady buzz of CNN, BBC, PBS television cameras

Correspondents from AP. AFP, Reuters, El Mundo, all straining to be recognized.

Here goes" whispered the teenage focus of all the press attention. "Here, I go."

"Yes, Honey" coaxed Sister Aimée, gently. *"Be not afraid.* I know you will make us all at St. Elisabeth's rightly proud!"

"I hope so."

For any newcomer to celebrity, the glare of television floodlights, the burst of newspaper camera flashbulbs and the jabbering of reporters could certainly be intimidating. To find reassurance, Sister Jeanne recited silently from **Psalm 25**: *"To you O Lord I lift up my soul. O my God I trust in You. Let me not be ashamed. Let not my enemies triumph over me. Indeed, let no one who trusts in You be ashamed."*

Clearly, God answered the plea.

If she begun at halting pace, the girl who journalists were so dying to meet, soon recovered her resolve and took command.

"Sister Jeanne?"

"Yes, Madame."

"Are you pleased with the worldwide appeal of your writings?"

"Oh yes indeed, Madame! I love history and literature. These subjects are super awesome! I am delighted to learn that so many others share my conviction. If my writings do anything to further expand the world's interest in history and literature, I will realize I've done my sacred duty. I will know my books and articles proved to be of at least some minor consequence. I will know that I've contributed at least a slight measure of good to our troubled world."

Snap, snap, snap, snap, snap snap–additional newspaper photographer snaps.

"Remember my friends" continued Sister Jeanne, "*Literature* is not merely a set of thick, old tomes gathering dust on a library shelf. *Literature* is something far greater than a compilation of famous but dull authors you only read because teacher instructs you must in order to pass your Bacho. No, no! *Literature:* from Homer to Solzhenitsyn, from Sappho to Akhmatova–I'm not as acquainted with more contemporary authors but they count, too–each, all, beautifully, matchless record all the passions, the hopes and dreams of the human soul."

"To enjoy *literature*" insisted Sister Jeanne, employing her outstretched arms for emphasis, "is to both appreciate and to understand the human psyche. If *Literature* were a river, it would be broader than the Missouri, longer than the Nile, more powerful than the Amazon. Why: **I'll wait to see the movie–w**hen you can instead embrace the tale in all its original truth and majesty!"

Emotion twirled her like a ballerina or Olympic figure skater high in the air.

"Are any pieces of literature that are your particular favorites?"

"I've always enjoyed *The Romance of Tristan and Iseult*" responded Sister Jeanne. "It's probably Western Civilization's original love story. First placed on paper by an unknown scribe in the early Twelfth Century, the saga already dated in verbal form to several hundred years earlier.

"Almost a millennium before Marvin Gaye sang: "*There is no mountain high, no valley low*" explained Sister Jeanne, "Tristan and Iseult pledged: **Neither fortress, nor tower, nor royal prohibition shall keep me from the call of my lover whether it be wisdom or folly.**"

Snap, snap, snap, snap, snap snap–additional newspaper photographer snaps.

"The same, my friends, is true of history!" added Cherie. "*History* is not just a pile of old, heavy volumes amassing cobwebs on a library shelf. *History* is something far greater than a list of dates and a set of events teacher instructs us to remember in order to pass our Bacho. *History*

90

is–his–or **her–story!** Remember, nothing *had* to happen. But it did happen nonetheless. We should concentrate not so much on *when, where* and *how* as on *why* and then: *why not this instead.* From the invention of writing to the invention of the Internet, from pyramids to spaceships, *History* records the yearnings, hopes and dreams of humanity! And far better than fiction, too!"

"Suppose" explained the young nun as if she now become the teacher of a grammar school class, "you went to Hollywood with a script about a girl named Joan of Arc. Movie-makers would instantly dismiss the story as 'too melodramatic for anyone to take seriously.' But don't forget, Joan of Arc and her remarkable story actually happened! See! Truth is so often stranger than fiction. That's why *History* is such a super awesome thing to study. One, everybody should adore! If you don't feel as I do it's simply because you were taught the subject purely! But I digress."

Snap, snap, snap, snap, snap snap–additional newspaper photographer snaps.

"Sister Jeanne?"

"Yes, Monsieur?"

"When did you first begin to write?"

"Oh, from the moment I learned to scratch letters on a page."

"And why writing, Sister Jeanne?"

"Why writing, Madame? And not say, figure skating? God provides His creatures various gifts. Some He makes born to be artists; others to be scientists; some to dance; some to hit a ball. God chose me to write."

"How do you decide what to write, Sister Jeanne? And then, how much time do you devote to it daily?"

"Basically, ideas and the ability to put them on paper properly, just come." the author confessed. "I'm sorry I can't be more specific. Of course, sometimes they both just **don't come** and then, I'm stuck– On occasion, for weeks. It's true that people like Mama–she now in Heaven–or here at St. Elisabeth's: Abbess Marie and Sister Francoise–"

She threw her patronesses warm, grateful kisses.

"–can point me in a fruitful direction, can offer me good advise and fine encouragement. Ultimately, however, an idea and my ability to .put it on paper just needs to come. I know that's a vague answer to your question but likely most other writers will tell you the same thing."

"Do you plan writing more, Sister Jeanne?"

"Oh, yes of course, my friends.

"And when will readers get to enjoy your next book, Sister Jeanne?"

"I can't tell for sure" responded the virgin chronicler. "It will be in the coming year, I promise. But I can't tell you exactly what month and day. Remember as I told you earlier my friends, writing comes when it comes. As the author, I am like every artist, or to paraphrase Simone Weil, 'merely the instrument of a higher power.'"

"I can assure you though, my friends" she guaranteed, "that another book or set of articles for you to read and hopefully also enjoy is definitely on the way. I've just got to get my creative juices bubbling in the proper way."

Is there any piece of art you particularly like, Sister Jeanne?"

"The Winged Victory of Samothrace."

"Is there any piece of music you enjoy in particular?

"The violin concerto by Dvorak in A Minor."

"Why those two works especially, Sister Jeanne?"

"See and listen to them and you'll at once know why."

"Can we quote you on that, Sister Jeanne?"

"Yes, you may, for whatever my opinion is worth."

"When did you first sense you possessed a religious *Calling*, Sister Jeanne?"

"From age four or five."

"What did that religious *Calling* feel like, Sister Jeanne?"

"It's hard to describe. It's like the Winged Victory of Samothrace or the violin concerto by Dvorak. Ultimately, nothing that beautiful can be transposed into mortal words. I just knew from the first that Christ selected me to be His bride. I simply knew from the first that I'd never be happy or feel fulfilled, that I'd never think I'd done my duty as a believer until I obeyed His wish to let Him take me as His own."

"Do you also follow *Pop* culture, Sister Jeanne?"

"When Sister Barbara cried: 'Someone shot John!' I didn't need to ask *John* who?"

"Are there any songs by John Lennon you like in particular, Sister Jeanne?"

"*Blackbird* and *Revolution*."

"*Revolution!*" responded the reporters. "You mean from *The White Album?*"

"Yes, my friends. From *The White Album!*"

"I also like Bob Dylan" she volunteered. "Especially, *Mister Tambourine Man*."

"*Hey, Mister Tambourine Man, play a song for me, I'm not sleepy and*—"the nun's soft, melodic voice intoned the famous ballad.

Gently, Sister Jeanne wearing her long black habit and white wimple, danced in graceful step about the chapel.

The sound of her gentle step and mellifluous voice echoed up into the 40-meter *Gothic* vault

That tune and accompanying dance complete, the nun added: "I like Carole King, too! Carole King makes me; *"Feel like a natural woman!*

Her eyes closed and arms raised in pensive ecstasy, the virgin in long black habit and white wimple again gently danced in elegant step about the chapel.

She intoning softly: "—*It makes me feel like a natural woman!*"

Snap, snap, snap, snap, snap snap—additional newspaper photographer snaps.

"Sister Jeanne, are you a Feminist?"

"If by *feminist*, you mean—'Am I for unisex bathrooms; do I think women shouldn't shave their legs; do I object to letting the guy pick up the check; do I think actresses ought to be called 'actors?' then no, I am not. If on the other hand, by *feminist* you mean—"Do I believe that women should receive equal pay for equal work; that women should be rewarded as much as men for their intellectual and artistic accomplishments; that Mamas should be honored for their nurturing; that women should be provided an equal chance with men to achieve success in this world?" Then, yes, I am and have always have been a *feminist*."

"Has this girl ever considered running for public office!" whispered one reporter to another. "Socialist or Conservative, Communist or Monarchist, I've no doubt she'd get elected!"

Snap, snap, snap, snap, snap snap—additional newspaper photographer snaps.

"So, are you a supporter of Mrs. Thatcher, too?"

"As a woman, yes." replied Sister Jeanne.

"And of Madame Merkel?"

"As a woman, yes."

"Are you for artificial birth control?"

Sister Jeanne paused introspective.

"Having never once known—having never once experienced being with man in that way—as today, I being a nun under *Solemn Vows*—I don't believe I am justified in giving an opinion on that subject."

The queries from the press corps now followed in rapid succession—

"Should Hilary stop putting up with Bill?"

"Should pot be decriminalized?"

"Do you favor giving refugees citizenship?"

"Do you endorse *Gay Marriage*?"

"Are you for *Reparations*?"

"How can humanity best confront *Global Warming*?"

"Do you think women in Saudi Arabia ought to be allowed to drive?"

"Aren't we here to discuss my writing, my friends?" observed Sister Jeanne, fending off the media's effort to catch her in a gaffe. "I thought you wished to meet me, to let my readers discover who I am."

She smiled demure.

Batted her eyes.

Curtseyed deep.

"Thank you very much for coming this morning Messieurs and Mesdames" abruptly cut-in Sister Aimée. "This interview is now closed. Any further reasonable questions you have for The Child on literature, art and history and on her life as a religious will be responded to in full, in short time, and in writing by me from St. Elisabeth's press office. The sisters of St. Benedict are all deeply touched and grateful for your interest in The Child. 'May the peace of God who's mystery surpasses all understanding be amongst you now and remain with you always.'"

V

"Wonderful! Wonderful!" extolled Mother Marie after she and her buddy since Sunday School took Sister Jeanne back into the cloister. "You were splendid Cherie! Magnificent! I bet a lot of those people are now rushing off to the Internet to look up a photo of The Winged Victory! I bet the sales of Dvorak recordings are now leaping through the roof!"

"You were brilliant, Sweetheart!" cried Sister Francoise. "You were tremendous, Honey! Positively all that we could ever hope of you!"

"And more!" added Mother Marie.

"*Arise shine for thy light has come*" cried Sister Francoise, quoting **Isaiah**: "*and the glory of the Lord has risen upon thee.*"

"*Then you shall see and be radiant*" exclaimed Mother Marie, she also quoting **Isaiah**: "*:your heart shall thrill and rejoice.*"

"Ooo! Ooo!"

"Goodness gracious!"

"Praise the Virgin!"

"Yes, praise the Virgin!"

"The *Two Lovelies* held Sister Jeanne tight. They showered their pet with heartfelt kisses; next, the duo jumped up-and-down in place with Darling in her patroness's arms. The two nuns and their mutual Bundle of Joy only came to a halt when all three were thoroughly exhausted.

"What a statesman–*stateswoman* Cherie was, *is*" commented Mother Marie, gasping for breath, though as Abbess, she was sure to maintain her ladylike manners.

"Yes, a *stateswoman*" endorsed Sister Francoise, gasping for breath though as Sub-Abbess, she was sure to maintain her ladylike manners.

"Those silly scribblers tried all they could to maneuver The Child into making a gaffe, into saying something controversial. Yet Baby successfully parried them each time!

"So, The Child did!"

"Ooh! Ooh!

"Goodness gracious!"

"Praise the Virgin!"

"Yes, the Virgin be praised!"

"I'm pleased my superiors think that I comported myself well" confided Sister Jeanne. "It was my first time outside the cloister in over two years. I wasn't sure I could handle all the media hoopla. I'm pleased to learn that my superiors judge my conduct was good."

Sister Jeanne paused.

A frown appearing on her pretty face.

"I wish so much people would stop calling me: *The Child*."

THE LOVER'S CALL

Time passed
Seasons changing
Ideas now more intricate.

"*S*ister Jeanne Navarro's latest creation: **A Woman's History of the Middle Ages** is a pure jewel!" asserted *Figaro*."It is a diamond" commented *Le Monde*."The Child's latest work is a masterpiece!" was heard the voice of Great Britain's *New Statesman*. "Yet again, the Child provides her avid and ever-growing readership with brilliant incites. All of them composed in a matchless literary style" wrote *The Washington Post*. "The Child's writing is superb" was the judgment of Italy's *Corriere Della Sara*.

Sister Jeanne became the youngest person ever chosen for both the *Prix de Goncourt* and the *Prix de Rome*. Immensely honored to receive awards only a few years earlier thought just a wild schoolgirl dream, the author nevertheless insisted her religious Vows obliged her to decline. "As yet a further mark of this remarkable Child's increasing cultural value" noted *Deutsche Zeitung*, "no runner-up was picked in the youngster's place." Said *The Guardian*: "No more simply just a cute prodigy, The Child has now firmly established herself as one of contemporary Europe's premier historians."

"I'm deeply honored to be selected for these awesome literary distinctions" commented Sister Jeanne humbly in one of the rare interviews she granted. This one, to *The Associated Press*. "Still, I so wish people would stop calling me–The Child."

I

St. Elisabeth's, September 2

My dearest Rose, let me congratulate you on your two splendid Olympic gold medals in Lisbon. You not only brought home for France victory in the 5,000 Women's Meters race but also in the 10,000 Women's meters race. In addition, you smashed the previous time and speed records! Goodness gracious! I saw you even lap all your opponents! Be it know that not only Sister Francoise and I but all the members of our convent watched the races on our television! Yes, nuns can on occasion watch television too! We are all so excited for you Rosalie. So excited. One of the perks about being an abbess is that I am entitled to instruct all my fellow sisters to make special prayers. I ordered them all to pray for you throughout the Lisbon games. Clearly, Our Lady, The Virgin both listened and responded to our calls. Bless you, bless your, bless you my darling, precious, triumphant, Olympian Rosalie.

Always with love, your cousin Marie OSB

P.S. I include with this letter a copy of Jeannette's newest book, I/m sure you will enjoy it immensely.

Mother Marie halted.

Her fetching face registered deep concern.

She bit her maternal lip.

The abbess hurriedly contributed addition words to her biweekly letter.

PPS. Fear not my dearest very own Rosalie. My love for you is not diminished in the slightest! If I had my way, I'd immediately bring you into my convent and kiss and hold you close forever! I simply wish you to read this fine book. You and Jeannette are both matchless little girls, It is my fondest wish that you kids get to know each other. I am confident you two will become the closest of buddies.

II

If *The Two Lovelies* were delighted with their gifted protegée's spiritual and intellectual development at St. Elisabeth's and literary critics from *Le Monde* of Paris to Tokyo's *Nihon Keizei Shinbun* sang Cherie's praises, the teenager herself was less certain. Both, of her personal value and its level of consequence to the world. A devout Roman Catholic of mystical persuasion, she was initially much attracted to a secluded life of prayer, contemplation and study. Yet while demonstrated she possessed both an unquestionable religious *Calling* and the skill to transform her thoughts into major, lasting, and highly compelling pieces of theology appealing to readers around the world, Sister Jeanne continued sensing that her true place and true mission were located elsewhere.

Famine in the Horn of Africa
Civil War in Latin America
Military coup in Southeast Asia
Dictatorship in Europe
Plague globally

"How" Cherie asked herself on repeated occasions, "am I to confirm the pledge I made to God on the mountain ridge if I remain in this convent?"

"How can I be God's comrade-in-arms, God's warrior" increasingly the girl pondered, "if I stay at St. Elisabeth's?"

At first, Sister Jeanne divulged her concern to not a soul. She confided her troubles not even to her patronesses and surrogate-parents: Mother Marie and Sister Francoise. "The only individuals privileged sharing any of the secret were the thought-provoking Fifteenth Century Fra Filipino Lippi murals and terracotta Della Robbia *bas reliefs* decorating the cross-beamed, vaulted chapel and the restful, Cordoba terraces which the solitary nun often paced in melancholy thought.

"*Be anxious for nothing, but in everything by prayer and supplication, with thanksgiving, let your requests be made known to God*"–advises **Philippians**. Nevertheless, that passage offered more relief when earlier, as Mademoiselle Juana Navarro, she sat atop the mountain ridge. Today's cloistered Sister Jeanne was in a far better position to transform her childhood passions, hopes and dreams into clear, visible, decisive action. As **1 Thessalonians** went on to remind her–"*We were well pleased to impart to you not only the gospel of God but our own selves.*" In **I Timothy**, St. Paul speaks of having: "*fought the good fight*" and of: "*having run the race.*" Had Sister Jeanne, too: "fought the good fight"? Had she, too: "run the race?" Naturally, in his own time, St. Paul did not expect such principles applied to women. However, much was altered in Western society and its view of acceptable sexual roles since the age of the Greeks and Romans.

Beseeching others either through word or in book to risk their own lives while she remained safely behind thick convent walls served only to fill the young nun with a near-palpable sense of guilt. If accepted sexual roles were much altered since Classical times, other human concepts like Honor and Responsibility were unchanged. "So, rather than me observing a life of pious self-denial" thought Sister Jeanne, "am I instead just fleeing my rightful duties in order to lead an existence of total self-absorption?"

As was made abundantly clear from both newspaper accounts and conversations with guests in the grilled Visitors Parlor, murder and mayhem continued to ravage the outside world unabated. Such dreary events persisted without Sister Jeanne's fervent prayers or her highly acclaimed books appearing to produce the slightest positive effect against them.

War in Africa
Religious persecution in China
Flood in India

Military coup in South America
Yet another 'once in a lifetime' hurricane in the United States
"So, is the *wunderkind* of the Pyrenees really just a coward?" she asked herself. Or worse still, a hypocrite? "Am I ultimately no better than the Levite in the *Parable of the Good Samaritan* in **Luke**? The person, who, tells the victim of highwaymen robbed, beaten, stripped and left to die naked, bloodied in the road that he can't provide assistance because he's in a hurry to go the temple in Jerusalem to praise God for making him such a pillar of virtue!"

Sister Jeanne loved her neighbor.

She desperately wished carrying-out this commandment in more than words.

At last, she could bear the self-reproach no longer.

She collapsed.

III

Ironically, some of Sister Jeanne's finest writing proved a major cause of her nervous breakdown. The critically-acclaimed, bestselling history she wrote about Benedictine nuns brought to public attention many ladies who were noted philosophers, scientists, diplomats, painters, creative writers, composers, sculptors, even singers. All, were fascinating individuals who in a different time and place would doubtless freely offer their unique gifts to a larger world. Each, was a lady who's contribution to society was for too long either ignored or shamelessly minimized. Today, the public routinely benefited from the scientific theories, practical inventions, art works, even historic changes for which these ladies were responsible, often without any contemporary knowledge of who brought them about. To this list of unsung heroines, the author included her two patronesses.

Most of those destined for a religious life, Sister Jeanne explained, adjusted to its confines and found contentment in this restricted if also safe environment. Likely, a good number would never discover their special abilities if they become traditional wives and mothers.

Nevertheless, most did not take the veil as a first choice; and if the convent sometimes ignited gifts inhabits didn't previously know they possessed, the cloister was also responsible for keeping news of such intellectual or artistic achievements long unknown.

Rather than making Sister Jeanne rightly proud, publication of her newest work (first appearing as an essay series in the *Two Lovelies'* journal *Faith Today* and later available in bestselling book form), projected Sister Jeanne into tangled, knotted, labyrinthine depression. Soon, the girl stopped eating. She began to twitch, shiver, and stutter. She vomited blood, developed insomnia. After a few days, she became unable to stand or relieve herself unassisted. Following a week of watching the youngster's steady physical and mental decline, the Abbess and Sub-Abbess ordered their star correspondent restricted to the convent infirmary. Medical and psychological experts were summoned from Pau to oversee Darling's care.

Bishop Yves Gautier asked the nuns at St. Elisabeth's to please keep him regularly informed of how events developed. As arguably the man most responsible for persuading Mademoiselle Navarro to embark on the journey she took, the Bishop felt a special accountability for her welfare. "It's our personal duty to make sure this unique Sweetheart is not lost to the world!" urged His Grace to the Abbess. "The Child offers a holy benefit to each of us! A Dear like her comes around only once in an age!"

"Didn't Virginia Woolf kill herself after completing a book?" queried Mother Marie, greatly distressed.

"Yes, indeed, she did!" answered Sister Francoise, also much worried, "Remember, John Stuart Mill suffered a similar collapse at Jeannette's age?"

"I guess our own John Stuart Mill is suffering in the same way. And at least the first J.S. Mill was a boy. Such a heavy load of brains must be terribly hard for only a girl to manage."

"We must be ever watchful of The Child," insisted Mother Marie. "We can't permit our Jeannette to do something foolish! History would never forgive our rash, stupid oversight."

"We must keep our Jeannette close at all times," endorsed Sister Francoise.

Not for an hour either during day or night was the girl allowed to be alone.

Hoping "Our Lady, The Virgin might chip in her own immaculate hand where vexed-human medical knowledge fails," Mother Marie ordered that all the sisters at St. Elisabeth's contribute special daily prayers for Cherie's recovery.

"What true good have I ever contributed to this sinful world, myself?" the young author thought, lying beneath her bed in the infirmary. In the air, she smelt that clean, antiseptic, bleach-like aroma particular to all care facilities. The patient's bed sheets were arranged in that precise, exact manner only nurses know how to perform. Sister Adele, Sister Caroline and Sister Penny alternated in being stationed nearby to make sure their fellow nun didn't "try to do something stupid to herself."

Even with her body now immobile and her mind clogged with heavy clinical sedatives, Miranda's daughter could still differentiate between the seeming important and the apparent trivial. "Historians after all" she ventured silently, "only deliver judgments on the actions of others far greater and more bold than themselves! No one would ever hear of me hadn't others far better than me come first to do things I might later dare comment on.

"Are you feeling alright, Darling?" asked Sister Penny Ramirez, suspecting anxiety in the invalid's troubled expression. A former University of Southern California *Flower Child* who threw away much of her own highly gifted youth by taking dope and parading about in *Summers of Love*, Sister Penny was both deeply appreciative and ever protective of remarkable adolescent Cherie. This talented girl, was not at all unlike Sister Penny at her own age. "Is there anything I can do for you, Jeannette? Remember, I know more than a thing or two about being a kid addled in the head. Can I possibly help, give advise?"

The invalid motioned with her eyes that loving guardian need not worry.

"Well be sure to rest, relax, Dear. Further high, noble thoughts can wait till later" urged Sister Penny, she applying gentle strokes to the invalid's thick, silky, brown . "Leave searching for a way to fix this troubled world until later. In the meantime, we all want our little sage to return to us recovered in soul as well as in body!"

Sister Penny gave the invalid a tender kiss on her forehead.

The invalid responded with a grateful press of guardian's right hand.

"Who am I to cast judgment on my fellow Benedictine sisters in centuries passed?" muttered Sister Jeanne, lying in her hospital bed, head groggy with medical sedatives. "After all, I was not banished or exiled to a convent. Instead, I chose it of my own free will! Me! Who knew I already possessed both writing skill and a religious *Vocation* from childhood! Me! I, who unlike many of those in my book, did not need to discover my gifts only following years of personal struggle, after years of mental turmoil while confined in a place I did not chose to be!"

"I'm no philosopher" she averred. "I'm no scientist. I'm no painter, no inventor, no diplomat, no composer. All I do is comment on the achievements of others! People praise me, admire me. Yet all I really do is reflect on others deeds."

"In the end" thought the girl beneath the hospital sheets, her head groggy, "I'm just a scribbler who–"

"Hush!" ordered maternal Sister Penny, "rest Dear, rest!"

Again, she gently kissed the invalid's troubled forehead.

The patient responded with a grateful press of her guardian's right hand.

Twisted thoughts in the little theologian's head?

Perhaps.

Maybe, severe introspection is always a bit twisted in nature?

At least, Sister Jeanne had now reached the bottom of of her despair.

From here, no direction existed but up.

IV

"*Behold, You desire truth in the inward being*" pleaded Miranda's daughter, the girl quoting from **Psalm 51**, "*therefore teach me wisdom in my secret heart.*"

"That's absolutely correct, Jeannette"–interjected Lover.

"Bless you! Bless you!" answered Soul mate, overjoyed by her amorous protector's sudden intercession.

"Now get a-hold of yourself, Jeannette sweetheart"–gently admonished Lover. "Remember when you spoke so well to the press?"

"Yes, I recall the episode, Darling."

"Cherie said that I give out different skills to different people."

"So indeed, I did, Honey."

"To some, Jeannette, I give the ability to paint, to others I grant the skill to invent, to others. the talent to sculpt."

"To yet others Lord, You make inventors, diplomats, singers, teachers."

"Precisely, Cherie! Well, I've granted my personal sweetheart the gift of being a brilliant author."

"Bless you, my Dearest!" answered Lover's faithful companion, tears no longer in the teenager's thoughtful gray-green eyes.

"So cut-out this silly whining and disgraceful self-pity, my Jeannette!" counseled her transcendent Lover. "I've granted Darling a gift. She must now use it to the full–Just as I intended Darling to do. All those Benedictines from the past are depending on you. Without your skilled pen, they would be almost totally forgotten by the contemporary world, Honey. So stop feeling sorry for yourself and get back to work–Get back to work being the historian I've decided Cherie is meant to be."

Sister Jeanne sat up, a new surge of creative, confident energy running both her mind and body. "Bless you Lord! When I was at my lowest you came to nourish me, to clothe me, to preserve me."

"That's my job"–advised Lover. "It's my job to look out for you."

Miranda's daughter rose from her hospital bed, refreshed as never before.

"So off you go Jeannette, my comrade in arms!" –urged Lover.

"Where next am I to take my writing?" inquired the former invalid. "Where next? I'm beginning to think St. Elisabeth's is becoming too narrow."

"You might well be right, my little warrior"–answered Lover. "It might indeed be time for Darling to move on."

"Move on, Lord?" asked Soul mate, hopefully. "You wish me to *move on?*"

"Yes, Jeannette sweetheart. It is time for you to expand the horizons of your ambition. The day is coming for you to spread your writing all about the world. I know many people in many countries are waiting to receive it. Demonstrate through your pen how the solemn Vows you took can benefit the entire world."

MISSION

....

Time passed
Issue arose
Problems were resolved
Or so, at least it appeared

"*I* must go now, Mama" confided Daughter to Mother, the latter resting in grave under a wide evergreen tree in convent garden. Beneath her veil, Sister Jeanne's thick, silky, brown locks were now grown back to beneath her shoulders. "It is time I must move on. Duty calls me. But don't worry. I won't forget you. I promise, Mama, I'll make you proud of me."

Now recovered from her mysterious illness, Sister Jeanne resumed her regular conversations with Miranda. These were encounters with her parent, the girl was sure to perform every day following Morning Prayer save when it heavily snowed or rained. Spring was returned and the foliage at St. Elisabeth's was once more in full bloom. Famous since before the Revolution, these expansive flowerbeds expertly designed and well maintained since long ago, each year without fail, offered local residents a veritable ocean of:: roses, tulips, hollyhocks, irises, pansies, delphiniums, phlox, anemones, petunias, forsythias, lilies of the valley, scillas, camellias, hyacinths, magnolias and crocus. All swaying back-and-forth in gentle, majestic unison like waves of the sea, this celebrated mass of flowers transform themselves into a sea of God's pure, brilliant, voluptuous rainbow color.

White
Red
Orange
Yellow
Violet
Blue
Purple
Green–each, all, projected at most grand and beckoning.

"I've got a mission to undertake now, Mama" explained Sister Jeanne. "One, I must take to many foreign lands. I've felt this was my mission long before I ever arrived at *St. Elisabeth's*. I've known this is my mission almost from the first time I stood on the ridge back at San Pedro and first spoke with my Special Chum atop the cloud wreathed mountain top."

She paused.

"Even back then, Mama, I knew God chose me as his Comrade-in-Arms. Even back then, Mama, I knew God chose me as his Little Warrior. So, it's time now I got started on the path to which I'm called."

"There's no more time for dithering" concluded Sister Jeanne, "I must get started." She then quoted from **Romans**: *"It is reckoned of us who believe."*

I

Of course, Sister Jeanne first still needed to obtain the permission of her superiors. And considering he fuss Mademoiselle Navarro made to enter St. Elisabeth's and taking into account the literary distinction she brought the convent once she was accepted, wouldn't *The Two Lovelies* raise objection to her now leaving? Even, if in departing, she sought not to renounce her religious Vows but simply wished exercising those same duties on a larger stage? "If Cherie has prayed about this decision long and hard, if Cherie sincerely believes God wishes her to embark on this mission" wrote Bishop Gautier, "I will naturally back Sweetheart to the full." Judging, however, that he already interfered more than enough in the Church's regular chain-of-command, His Grace continued: "Still, I don't believe it is right for me to personally intervene. An issue of this kind is properly settled within your own religious Order and by its local authorities." Lest the girl lose heart, though, Gautier assured her: "I know that like yourself, the abbess of St. Elisabeth's and her chief assistant are also each highly intelligent, very talented and quite open-minded individuals. If Cherie puts her case to them succinctly and with respect, I am confident a settlement favorable to all ladies involved can be be reached."

"Yes, His Grace is correct" thought Sister Jeanne after reading Bishop Gautier's letter. "I owe it to my patronesses to explain myself. I don't want to appear like one of those full-of-herself-types or be considered a head-in-the-clouds flibbertigibbet. In addition, it's my duty to show my superiors the obedience and respect they are both each owed and deserve."

She paused.

"Finally, I need to know I carry with me their blessing. I need to know I carry with me their love and prayers."

I

"Are you sure this is what you truly want, Jeannette?" queried Mother Marie.

She motioned for her protegée to sit on wise big friend's lap

"Ooh! You're still so light, Cherie! I could almost raise Jeannette with a single arm!" commented Mother Marie, with fond concern. "Please make sure to eat all your required nutrition, protein and Vitamin C! Being a great author means Sweetheart needs a strong, healthy body as well as a creative, searching mind! Remember, we took Vows to serve God not to try and make ourselves look like Auschwitz survivors!"

Along the papered walls of Abbess's office were framed color photos of both her track star cousin Raymonde capturing two Golds at the

Lisbon Olympics and of Sister Jeanne, she first delivering a lecture and later receiving the news of winning the *Prix Goncourt*. The teenagers were the same age. If Abbess was in fact just nine years older, she nevertheless regarded the talented pair as her own sacred responsibilities, if not children.

"I must be sure The Child wears these correctly" said Abbess silently to herself. First sartorial job complete, she next, set to work readjusting the position of sidekick's *Crucifix* and *Rosary*."Yes," she further said under her breath, "I must see to it that Jeannette looks proper."

"Are you really sure this is what you want, Jeannette?"repeated Mother Marie, this time in audible voice. She fiddling with the angle of the young author's habit. "You truly wish to leave St. Elisabeth's? I thought you were so happy and fulfilled here? You've never mentioned any loneliness or spiritual suffering you've undergone. The superb articles and books you wrote demonstrate that life at St. Elisabeth's? has been crucial to your intellectual and artistic development!"

She paused, growing anxiety on her lovely face.

"Considering all that Jeannette has achieved at St. Elisabeth's—both for herself and for her entire Order—is she absolutely certain taking this jump into the unknown is the correct move to now take? If something bad happens to Sweetheart, the responsibility for allowing it to occur rests squarely with Abbess. Therefore, Abbess must be convinced it is a risk worth taking!"

"And are you fully recovered from your terrible illness, Jeannette?" interjected no less uneasy Sister Francoise, until now standing silent at Mother Marie's left. "Is Jeannette's wish to leave us in any way influenced by poor health? As your superiors, it would be very wrong of us to permit you setting out when you are only half-well. Never forget, poor health might well be effecting Jeannette's otherwise so clear judgment."

For *The Two Lovelies*, who each believed the cloister provided women infinitely more intellectual and emotional independence, offered women far wider freedom of action than was ever available in the male-dominated eat-or-be-eaten "larger" world, Sister Jeanne's request to leave could not but sound ill-conceived.

"Might Jeannette be intending–" anxiously started to question Sister Francoise.

Before her soulmate could finish the dreadful sentence, Mother Marie supplied the expected foreboding words. "–to renounce her religious Vows? Is she planning to toss aside the pledges she made to Christ and to the Blessed Virgin? If this be so, a usually so devote, in regular times a so God-fearing child like Jeannette is obviously not today in her right mind. Without doubt, The Child is still suffering from a fever twisting her normally so cogent thoughts. No! No! No! Once again, no! Abbess strenuously refuses to permit you to ramble off on this foolish, insane escapade. When at last recovered, Child will dearly thank her Superior for not consenting to allow this mad escapade."

"In addition" she declared, "Abbess orders you be returned to the infirmary at once! Until further notice! Abbess instructs that you be kept under close watch! Both night and day" As clear symptom of Mother Marie's intense worry, the tone and cadence of her mellifluous voice, the language she chose when addressing sidekick, it grown in recent months so intimate, motherly, abrupt shifted back to the earlier formalized, distant fashion she used toward the girl when Bishop Gautier pressured Mademoiselle Navarro's acceptance into the community against its leader's will.

"Do I wish to give up my Vows! No! No! Certainly not, Mother!" at once replied Sister Jeanne. Jumping off wise, big friend's lap, she proceeded to stamp her right foot, grimace, bite lip, shake her fists in the air to provide all possible emphasis. "Certainly not, Mother! I am not suffering a fever! I am also not nuts! Nor, do I have any feverish or nutty ideas. When I took my Vows, I did so freely and with no purpose of evasion. I took them for life! When Sister Francoise promoted me to full, voting member of the Benedictine Order, I was ever-so pleased! I gladly accepted the honor. I happily embraced the position and all its duties and responsibilities. I did so freely, eagerly and with every intention of obeying them for life!

"That's something I'm delighted to learn!" answered Mother Marie. She, sighing with deep relief, her voice growing once more intimate, maternal.

."I am not feverish or nuts!" repeated Sister Jeanne, again stamping her right foot, again grimacing, biting her lip, waving clinched fists in the air. "I don't intend to abandon the Order. I simply feel called upon by God to spread our message beyond our convent. I wish to be more than an author who just comments on dangerous decisions, risky actions undertaken by far braver others. I sincerity feel called upon to do more than just chronicle events from the safety of the comfortable sideline! I want to be an active participant in the events about which I write. I describe! I think it only right to put my own neck in possible jeopardy. The Virgin be praised! Amen!"

The chum on the mountain's comrade-in-arms, special warrior, halted to refresh her lungs.

She then continued no less zealous in her presentation.

"I feel God wishes me to transform the words I put on paper into assertive, concrete action!" In the process of replying to her surrogate parent in so firm a manner, the girl's own tone and cadence of voice, choice of words also grew uncommonly aloof. Rather than an idealistic young nun in a convent wishing to set out on mission, she sounded instead like a lawyer in a courtroom or an office-seeker on the hustings.

"When I complete my service in the world" Sister Jeanne promised, "I will return directly to St. Elisabeth's. You will from then on hear no more of my *feverish, nutty talk* again. I simply ask for permission to undertake my–as you say– my *escapade*. I promise that actions I hope now to perform will bring just as much honor to our Order as does my current writing!'

Sister Jeanne again halted to catch her breath.

"Just watch me, Mother Marie! Just watch me, Sister Francoise! Give me this one chance to venture outside and you will never regret it! Our entire Order will never regret it! I wish to undertake this–*escapade*–not to have some *feverish, nutty* fun but because God calls me!"

Looking her superiors' directly in the eye with a certainty she never earlier displayed, the youngster concluded: "Trust me Mother Marie! Trust me Sister Francoise! You will never regret permitting me to do this!"

Rather than concluding by again stamping her foot or waving her clinched fists, the supplicant instead chose quoting from **1**

Thessalonians—"We *are determined to share with you not only the gospel of God but our own selves.*"

"Phew!" muttered Sister Jeanne muttered silent, she bending over exhausted, resting hands on her knees. "I better stop! I'm starting to repeat myself. I'm starting to sound, as Mama would say: 'Like a broken record.' Well, His Grace Bishop Gautier told me that if I present my case in a straight, fair, respectful manner I might win the day. I hope I did as His Grace suggested."

The girl's superiors listened to her oration silently and in a thoughtful, serious fashion.

Following the speech's completion a quiet moment elapsed.

A second instance of unspoken debate transpiring

Yet, a third.

Songbirds beyond open window chirped merry.

A ray of May sun illuminating softly the entire room.

The air was pleasantly cool.

"Let me and Francoise think about it, Cherie" at last pronounced the Abbess in slow, pondering tone. "Let my friend and I discuss your request alone for a time."

"When we are done" instructed Sister Francoise, "you will be called back to hear our decision."

"And in the meantime" instructed the Abbess, "don't discuss this matter with anyone. Not a living soul! Raise the matter only in your prayers."

"You've already begun writing your next set of essays for publication, have you not, Jeannette?" questioned Sister Francoise.

"Indeed, Sister" replied the celebrated young author. "I am going to call this latest set 'A woman's history of the Renaissance.' These will be a continuation of my earlier 'A woman's history of the Middle Ages.' Naturally, I will have them all appear first in our *Faith Today.*"

"Splendid! Splendid!" commented Mother Marie. "So, off you go, our sweet, loyal Jeannette! While your superiors debate your plea, you go back to proving yourself the fine writer and great historian the entire world is starting to recognize you to be."

II

Tap, tap, tap, tap, tap-of meditative adolescent sneakers traveling hall.

"What did it mean?" debated Sister Jeanne. "What did it mean?"

Further: tap, tap, tap, tap, tap-of meditative adolescent sneakers traveling hall.

"They didn't say **Yes**" observed the girl."But then again, they also didn't say **No**."

Creek, screech, whine, bump, slam, bang

"Ah! Finally done it at last!" Using both hands, our heroine succeeded in opening the thick mahogany door to the archives. After stopping a moment to catch her breath, she entered the vast chamber to resume her literary work. **A woman's history of the Renaissance –by Sister Jeanne Navarro OSB**. "I guess the best thing for me to do is get back to writing" she commented. "It doesn't seem as if I'll get an answer to my request for a couple days, maybe even longer. Getting back to work is the best way to stop my worries, stop my jitters." She paused reflective. "Anyway as Mother Marie is so fond of reminding me–*Rome wasn't built in a Day.*"

III

Time passed

A further cycle of days, elapsing

No decision on Sister Jeanne's request of her superiors was yet announced.

In meantime, the girl kept busy with her latest writing. Each day she spent countless hours seated atop the wicker chair, hunched over the long oak table in the vast, slightly musty archive chamber. Thanks to the wide appeal of Cherie's earlier books, the archive's oldest and most fragile document were now safely recorded on videotape.

Scratch, scratch, scratch, scratch of teenage pen to paper echoing chamber.

"Goodness! Gracious!" exclaimed Sister Jeanne upon discovering her present writing instrument run dry. "Another one is finished!" A moment later, taken a new pen from her khaki backpack resting nearby, she remarked: "I must be personally financing the entire French blue ink business!"

Additional: scratch, scratch, scratch, scratch —of teenage pen to paper echoing.

"So how is Jeannette's latest creation developing?" asked Sister Francoise, she recently tiptoed o the chamber to observe the convent's little genius at work.

"Oh, very well indeed Sister!"

Reaching across the oak table, the author picked up her latest finished piece.. It was composed in elegant, highly readable, feminine script and held together with a paperclip. "*Here,* Sister Francoise. Here, is the first essay of my new series to be published first in our journal *Faith Today.*"

"Brilliant! Brilliant!" exclaimed the pretty newcomer. "I'll see to it at once."

More time passed without a final verdict from the author's superiors.

Additional days, too.

Sister Jeanne completed a second essay for publication.

At last, she was summoned to the Abbess's office to hear the verdict.

IV

Mother Marie and Sister Francoise looked grave.

Each, stood erect, arms akimbo.

Both looked direct and with deep reflection at the incoming teenager.

The austere, silent expressions by of the *Two Lovelies* made protegée uneasy.

Was this girl about to be refused?

Her request turned down?

When first asking permission to journey outside, she had, as Bishop Gautier advised, presented her case in a respectful manner. What did she do wrong?

"Very well" pronounced Mother Marie, at last.. "Very well. Jeannette is given permission to travel—"

"For a certain period of time" Sister Francoise completed her chum's verdict.

"Bless you!:exclaimed the teenager. "Bless you both!"

The girl breathed with deep relief, her heart stopped palpitating.

She took a step forward to embrace her patronesses but Mother Marie instantly gestured for her ward to halt in place.

"Yes, Jeannette may temporarily travel outside the convent provided she is prepared accept several mandatory conditions."

"Yes, Mother Marie! What are these mandatory conditions I must accept?"

"First of all, Francoise and I don't wish to lose our brilliant little Cherie. We therefore expect you to mail us a weekly letter recording your activities—*in detail*. It is most important that we know precisely what our Darling is up to."

"Yes, I promise to do so."

"Second, we expect you to continue working on your next set essays and to mail each finished work back to us at St. Elisabeth's. You are after all a splendid author and the Order does not wish to lose your remarkable creative talent."

"Yes, Mother, I promise to do so as you wish."

"Good! Good!" commented *The Two Lovelies* writing their sidekick's answers on a sheet of lined yellow paper.

"You also intend to start your exploration from Paris, is that not correct?" queried Sister Francoise.

"Indeed I do, Sister."

"A trip across the country to a capital you've never previously visited being a long affair" explained Sister Francoise, "Marie and I wish you to be escorted."

A moment later, as if by earlier arrangement. the lady who guarded the invalid during her days in the infirmary entered the office.

"Sister Penny" inquired the Abbess, "you're from California, right?"

"Yes, I am, Mother" she answered, "San Francisco to be exact."

"Ooh! Wow! Cool! San Francisco!" chirped the Abbess with girlish delight, twirling her *Rosary*. "San Francisco! Say, do you know Nancy Pelosi?"

"Actually I did get to meet her a few times, Mother" answered Sister Penny Ramirez. "I know her kids much better, though. I went to both school and college with her youngest daughter."

"Well, if you're from California and know Nancy Pelosi, I'm sure you can also perform all this *Assertive Woman* stuff."

"'I'm sure you can also perform all this—*Assertive Woman stuff?*" giggled Sister Penny. "You aren't exactly a clinging-vine or a fragile hothouse flower yourself, Mother Marie!"

Thank you, Sister Penny. I try to set my community a good example to follow."

"Anyway" continued the Abbess, "I gave Sister Jeanne—*temporary*—permission to go outside the convent. She is traveling to Paris. Since Cherie never went to the capital before, I am instructing you to escort her there and make sure she gets in one piece to the Benedictine house in that city."

"Yes, Mother" answered Sister Penny. "I will do as you instruct."

"Just imagine Francoise!" piped Mother Marie in an aside to her soulmate since Sunday School. "Just imagine! Sister Penny knows Nancy Pelosi! Sister Penny knows Nancy Pelosi! Wow! Super! Awesome! No, *really* awesome!"

Once again the Abbess twirled her *Rosary.*

"Bless you! Bless you! Bless you all!" exclaimed Sister Jeanne, reaching out to embrace *The Two Lovelies* and shower them each with heartfelt hugs and tender kisses. Next, she took Sister Penny into her own arms. "I so adore and respect and look up to all three of you! I'm so grateful you give me this chance to prove myself to all the world! I promise, promise, promise you won't regret it! I promise, promise, promise I'll make you and the entire Order rightfully proud!"

"I pray to the Virgin it may be so, my darling Jeannette" answered Mother Marie, grown more pensive. She, at last freed herself from the teenager's desperate grasp. "May the Virgin look after you Sweetheart each and every day. I pray to all that is holy that I've just made the right decision."

SETTING OUT

$\mathcal{S}$o, following many tears and earnest pledges they soon return, Sister Jeanne and Sister Penny departed.

"Remember your promises!" wept the Abbess. "Remember to return when you've completed your missions! Your Mama is waiting anxiously for you to come back!"

"Come back as soon as you can, Sweethearts!" sobbed Sister Francoise. "Don't forget everyone at St. Elisabeth's loves you!"

The two nuns first stopped at Pau where they visited Bishop Gautier and Madame Arabaje.

"Out into the world you go" said His Grace to Sister Jeanne. "I'm so proud of you, Child." The Bishop kissed his young friend paternally on her forehead and quoted from **Psalm 118**: *"This is the day the Lord has made. Let us rejoice and be truly grateful."*

Then turning to Sister Penny, he whispered: "Make sure Cherie gets to Paris in one piece."

"My prayers are with you Dear" assured Auntie Maria. "I know my niece Miranda, now in Heaven, is ever so delighted with your brave endeavor.'

Next, the two nuns boarded a train and headed north. As they did so, the Pyrenees soon gave way to undulating, checkerboard agricultural land. This, periodically divided by winding midsize rivers and clumps of forest. Occasionally seen too, were cathedrals, monasteries, or hillside towns, all, each, existing since before the Crusades. In some directions:

animals contentedly munched the rich grass; in others: fields of wheat, rye and other crops swayed in gentle unison like waves of the sea. Had an intermittent farm truck or telephone pole not appeared, the scene beyond the speeding train window might be a pastoral work by Corot, Millet or Courbet.

"Look, Jeannette!" whispered Sister Penny to her young companion. "See what that man across the compartment is reading."

The author caught a surreptitious peek.

The traveler across the aisle was reading *Faith Today*.

"Do you like like that journal?" ventured the magazine's star reporter.

"Yes, indeed I do, Sister" responded the traveler, setting down the periodical. "I'm not a particularly religious man but I do so enjoy the articles written by this girl–pardon me, Sister–*young lady*–about women during the *Middle Ages* and now during the *Renaissance*. These articles she writes are so delightful to read, so insightful, so charming!" He paused. "This young lady is both a brilliant author and a superb historian!" He paused again. If a thoroughly secular individual, he was nevertheless careful to choose his words properly when addressing a nun, especially one so tender in age.

"I like those articles too, Monsieur" replied Sister Jeanne, with girlish pleasure. She only with great difficulty concealing her delight at this fellow passenger's approval of her own literary work.

The Gentleman was clearly unaware he now spoke to the articles' author.

"Do you by chance, belong to this young lady's same religious Order, Sister?"

"As a matter of fact I do, Monsieur" informed Sister Jeanne. "We are both Benedictines. The two of us also meet on occasion."

"Well, the next time you two good young ladies cross paths, be so kind as to convey my very high respect for her writing."

"Certainly, I will Monsieur. I definitely promise to tell her of your great praise."

"Will I perhaps be reading more work by this gifted writer in the coming months, Sister?" ventured the Gentleman.

"Oh, most assuredly you will, Monsieur" guaranteed Sister Jeanne. She only with difficulty concealing her immense delight at the approval of her literary work. "Another article about women during the *Renaissance* should be published by *Faith Today* in about a month."

"Excellent. I much look forward to reading the piece."

I

Upon the train reaching Paris at Gare Montparnasse, the two nuns collected their baggage, exited on to the platform, caught a taxi and proceeded into the center of the famous capital. It being **5:30 PM**, the thoroughfares, never empty, were at this hour particularly congested.

The taxi took a Right

A second, Right

Next, a Left,

Then, headed straight ahead north on the Boulevard St. Michel

"Do you Sisters mind if I listen to the radio?" inquired the cabby. The Olympics were being held that year in Frankfurt and the Final of the Women's Marathon was reaching its climax. "It looks as if–what does the press now enjoy calling her?–oh, yes, 'The Fleet-footed Duchess' is about to bring home yet another Gold for France."

"Yes, yes certainly keep the radio on, Monsieur" answered Penny. "My companion and I would be delighted to listen, too. Our Abbess is related to the racer."

"*This is history! This is history!*" proclaimed the radio announcer in choked, tearful, amazement. "*History is taking place before us. Nothing of this kind will probably ever happen again. Duchess Raymonde de Charpentier is about to become the greatest female long distance runner in history–perhaps the greatest female athlete of any kind! In fact, only one man: Emil Zatopek can boast a near equal accomplishment.*" The radio announcer stopped for a few seconds to cry before continuing his emotional oration. "*Having for yet a second time seized the Gold in the 5,000 meters–and broken her own record in doing so–having for yet a second time seized the Gold in the 10,000 meters–and broken her own record in ding so–the Fleet*

Footed Duchess de Charpentier is now about to also win the Marathon! The 5,000—a second time—the 10,000 meters—a second time—and now, also the Marathon! All three in the process of just six days! And just image! The Duchess de Charpentier never previously ran the Marathon! She simply decided today to make a goodhearted, ladylike attempt. And she won! She won! This is history, ladies and gentlemen! This is history! The Duchess de Charpentier has made herself the Caesar, made herself the Napoleon, the Roosevelt, the Michelangelo, the Beethoven, the Shakespeare of the track! The likes of Duchess de Charpentier will never, ever, come again!"

"Ooh!" exclaimed Sister Penny as Mother Marie's young cousin crossed the Finish line with all her competitors straggling far behind. "Abbess must now be dancing on air!"

"You said your Abbess is related to the Duchess de Charpentier, Sister?" asked the Cabby.

"Yes, Monsieur" replied Penny. "She and the Duchess are first cousins." The nun halted pensive. "The abbess of a famous convent and the winner of five historic Olympic golds! That's quite a distinction for any family in a single generation!"

"So it indeed is, Sister!" replied the cabby. "You must be rightly proud?"

"I am most mightily, Monsieur."

Vive La France!" all in the taxi cried.

The three broke into a hearty, full-throated rendition of **La Marseillaise.**

II

At last, the Boulevard St. Michel was traveled from south to north.

The vehicle next, crossed he murky Seine using the Pont Neuf.

Cabby then made a Right, next, a Left.

Driver and passengers crossed the Place Hotel de Ville where on August 25 1944, General de Gaulle proclaimed the Liberation.

Reaching the ever congested Rue Rivoli, the car next made a Right, a second Right, then sped direct ahead.

At last the destination was met.

III

For several days, Jeanne and Penny visited some of the city's many historic, cultural and artistic sites. They once even ate lunch at a restaurant where Simone Weil used to chat with Trotsky. The nuns' Vow of poverty, however, excluded they drop in at the Galleries Lafayette or at the boutiques on the Rue Rivoli.

Notre Dame, Louvre, Ile St. Louis, Ste. Chapelle, St. German-Auxerrois

Champ de Mars, Tour Eiffel, The Trocadero, Musée d'Orsay, Marmotton

Arche de Triomphe, Madeleine, Petit Palais, Place de Concorde, Invalides

Musée Cluny, St, Sevarin, Sorbonne, St. Etienne, Panthéon, Catacombs

Marais, Place Vendome, Hotel de Ville, St. Eustache, Centre Pompidou

St. Germain de Pres, St. Sulpice, Luxembourg Gardens, Jardin des Plantes

Montmartre, Sacré Coeur, St. Pierre, Pere Lachaise, St, Denis

Bois de Boulogne, Home of Colette, Longchamps, St. Germain-en-Laye

Versailles, Malmaison, Vincennes, Chantilly, Marly

And still so much more was left to be visited.

In their attempt to fully appreciate this magnificence, the two nuns almost walked their sneakers off. Upon arriving at the Petit Palais to see a new Modigliani exhibit, Penny nearly broke her right ankle when tripping on the slick marble stairs. Jeanne caught hold of her friend's arms just in time. Even the greatest beauty possesses dangers.

One evening after Penny recovered, she and Jeanne went to the Garnier Opéra to watch the prima ballerina Véronique Castellane perform *Firebird*. On a second date after sunset, the pair of Benedictines went to the University of Paris to attend a lecture by the great dancer's sibling Father Richard Castellane, recounting his most recent archeological expedition. On a a third nighttime outing, the nuns returned to the University of Paris to hear a talk Professor Matilda Eisenberg gave about her newest discoveries in the field of astronomy.

IV

"We've had a terrific time in Paris" said Penny the next morning. "However, it's time I start heading back to St. Elisabeth's. I pledged: 'to get Jeannette to the capital in one piece' and I've done so." She embraced her companion warmly. "From now on, Cherie must proceed on her mission alone. I've every confidence in Sweetheart's success. For she to succeed grandly! After all, your mission is our Order's mission, your mission is God's mission."

"Bless you, Penny" replied Sister Jeanne, returning the embrace. "Bless you Penny. Extend my thanks to all at St Elisabeth's when you get back! And to His Grace Bishop Gautier and to Madame Arabaje."

"I promise, Jeannette. Goodbye. I love you."

"Goodbye, Penny. I love you. too."

V

"So from that day forth" summarized Leopoldine Fauré to Mary Preston as the girls landed in France to begin their new life together, "Sister Jeanne Navarro went out to grasp the world."